A Tale of Two Kingdoms
(Black Swan 6)
Victoria Danann

Read more about this author and upcoming works at <u>VictoriaDanann.com</u>

Victoria Danann

Special THANK YOU'S...

Thank you to my assistants, Judy Fox and Sarah Nicole Blausey.

Thank you to Kelly Danann who gave me the confidence to publish the first book.

Thank you to Julie Roberts, world's best editor.

Thank you to my husband, my biggest cheerleader, who values every book sale and gets excited about every milestone.

Victoria is a big fan of the Black Swan A Team.

Anna-Marie Coomber
Anna Salamatin
Anne Rindfliesch
Brandy Ralston
Cheryl Lewis Fennimore
Cindy Hunt
Crystal Lehmann
Dee Bowerman
Diane Nix
Elizabeth Quincy Nix

Ellen Sandberg

Gina Whitney

Janine Fromherz Diller

Janna Ward

Jennifer Tracy

Karin Vaughan Sedor

Kim Staley Schommer

Laura E. Wolf

Laura Wright

Laurie Johnson

Laurie Peterson

Leah Barbush

Lindsay Thompson

Maggie Nolan

Merissa Sheppard

Mountain Crew

Nelta Baldwin Mathias

Pam James

Patricia Smith

Rebecca Stigers

Renay Arthur

Robyn Byrd

Rose Holub

Shanna Rankin

Shannon Cutrer Armstrong

Sharon Marcum

Shellie Stein

Susan Blanford Westerman

Sylvia Ashford
Tabitha Schneider
Talisa Martin
Ticia Morton Hall
Tifinie Henry

<u>PROLOGUE</u>

This series is also a serial saga in the sense that each book begins where the previous book ended. **READING IN ORDER IS <u>STRONGLY</u> RECOMMENDED** in order to fully enjoy the rich complexities of this tapestry in book form.

There is a very old and secret society of paranormal investigators and protectors known as The Order of the Black Swan. In modern times, in a dimension similar to our own, they continue to operate, as they always have, to keep the human population safe. For centuries they have relied on a formula that outlines recruitment of certain second sons, in their early, post-pubescent youth, who match a narrow and highly specialized psychological profile. Those who agree to forego the ordinary pleasures and freedoms of adolescence receive the best education available anywhere along with the training and discipline necessary for a possible future as active operatives in the Hunters Division. In recognition of the personal sacrifice and inherent danger, The Order bestows knighthoods on those who accept.

BOOK ONE. *My Familiar Stranger: The Vampire Hunters.*

The elite B Team of Jefferson Unit in New York, also known as Bad Company, was devastated by the loss of one of its four members in a battle with vampire. A few days later Elora Laiken, an accidental pilgrim from another dimension, literally landed at their feet so physically damaged by the journey they weren't even sure of her species. After a lengthy recovery, they discovered that she had gained amazing speed and strength through the cross-dimension translation. She earned the trust and respect of the knights of B Team and eventually replaced the fourth member, who had been killed in the line of duty.

She was also forced to choose between three suitors: Istvan Baka, a devastatingly seductive six-hundred-year-old vampire, who worked as a consultant to neutralize an epidemic of vampire abductions, Engel Storm, the noble and stalwart leader of B Team who saved her life twice; and Rammel Hawking, the elf who persuaded her that she was destined to be his alone.

BOOK TWO. *The Witch's Dream: Demon in the Details*

Ten months later everyone was gathered at Rammel's home in Derry, Ireland. B Team had been temporarily assigned to The Order's Headquarters office in Edinburgh, but they had been given leave for a week to celebrate an elftale handfasting for Ram and Elora, who were expecting.

Ram's younger sister, Aelsong, went to Edinburgh with B Team after being recruited for her exceptional psychic skills. Shortly after arriving,

Kay's fiancé was abducted by a demon with a vendetta, who slipped her to a dimension out of reach. Their only hope to locate Katrina and retrieve her was Litha Brandywine, the witch tracker, who had fallen in love with Storm at first sight.

Storm was assigned to escort the witch, who slowly penetrated the ice that had formed around his heart when he lost Elora to Ram. Litha tracked the demon and took Katrina's place as hostage after learning that he, Deliverance, was her biological father. The story ended with all members of B Team happily married and retired from active duty.

BOOK THREE. *A Summoner's Tale: The Vampire's Confessor*

Istvan Baka was captured by vampire in the Edinburgh underground and reinfected with the vampire virus. His assistant, Heaven McBride, was found to be a "summoner", a person who can compel others to come to them when they play the flute. She also turned out to be the reincarnation of the young wife who was Baka's first victim as a new vampire six hundred years before.

Elora Laiken was studying a pack of wolves hoping to get puppies for her new breed of dog. While Rammel was overseeing the renovation of their new home, she and Blackie were caught in a snowstorm in the New Forest. At the same time assassins from her world, agents of the clan who massacred her family, found her isolated in a remote location without the ability to communicate. She gave birth to her baby alone except for the company of her dog, Blackie, and the wolf pack.

Heaven was instrumental in calling vampire to her so that they could be intercepted and given the curative vaccine. Baka was found, restored, and given the opportunity for a "do over" with the wife who had waited for many lifetimes to spend just one with him.

BOOK FOUR. *Moonlight: The Big Bad Wolf*

Ram and Elora moved into temporary quarters at Jefferson Unit to protect mother and baby. Sol asked Storm to prepare to replace him as Jefferson Unit Sovereign so that he could retire in two years. Storm declined, but suggested twenty-year-old trainee, Glendennon Catch for the job.

Litha uncovered a shocking discovery about the vampire virus by accidentally leading five immortal host vampire back to Jefferson Unit. Deliverance struck a deal with Litha to assist Black Swan with two issues: the old vampire and an interdimensional migration of Stalkson Grey's werewolf tribe.

In the process of averting possible extinction of his tribe, the king of the Elk Mountain werewolves, Stalkson Grey, fell in love with a cult slave and abducted her with the demon's assistance. He eventually won his captive's heart and took his new mate to the New Elk Mountain werewolf colony in Lunark Dimension where the wolf people's ancestors had settled centuries before.

Throughout this portion of the story, Litha's pregnancy developed at an alarming rate. Since there had been no previous instance of progeny with the baby's genetic heritage, no one knew what to expect. The baby arrived months ahead of schedule. The birth was dramatic and unique because Storm's and Litha's new daughter, Elora Rose, "Rosie", skipped the usual delivery with a twelve inch ride through the passes and appeared on the outside of Litha's body.

BOOK FIVE. *Gathering Storm*

Book Five opened with Storm and Litha enjoying quiet days at home at the vineyard with a brand new infant. Sol shocked Storm with the news that he was getting married to Farnsworth and asked Storm to help Glen run Jefferson Unit so that he could take a vacation – his first ever – with his intended. Storm agreed, but when Rosie reached six weeks her growth began to accelerate drastically.

Deliverance was to pick Storm up every day, take him to Jefferson Unit so that he could spend two hours with Glen and supervise management of Sol's affairs, then return him to Sonoma, but the demon lost his son-in-law in the passes en route to New Jersey. Every paranormal ally available was called in for a massive interdimensional search. Finally, Deliverance was alerted that Storm had been located.

The demon picked him up and dropped him in Litha's bedroom, but it was the wrong Storm. B Team, Glen and Litha all undertook a project to do a makeover on the fake Storm so that nobody would find out that there was a huge flaw with interdimensional transport.

Jefferson Unit was attacked by aliens from Stagsnare Dimension, Elora's home world, with nobody there to offer defense except Elora, Glen, the fake Storm, Sir Fennimore, the non-combat personnel and the trainees.

NOTE for fans: If it's been a while since you've read the saga, this collection of references to events leading up to this installment is included as a "previously on" feature.

EXCERPT I *The Witch's Dream*

Though Aelsong had her back to the room, she kept getting the feeling that someone was staring. She finally turned to see who it was and her eyes locked on the navy blue gaze of a dark-haired angel sitting across the room. He didn't look away or try to hide the fact that he'd been staring. She let her eyes wander down his body and back up again before turning back to her group.

The pub had better food than Elora had expected. Everybody had eaten well and seemed to be having a good time. Well, everybody except Litha. Storm had decided to nip the pursuit in the bud by making a big show of flirting with an array of unattached women in the bar while ignoring her. Observing this, Elora concluded that he must be very afraid of Litha's potential power over him to engage in such un-Storm-like behavior.

Song also seemed more distracted than anything. Several times more she turned around to see what her admirer was up to. He was out with friends, raucous friends, but, whenever she turned his way, he stopped what he was doing and looked back like she was the only one in the room of any importance.

Out of nowhere someone yelled, "Elves!"

The music stopped. The talking stopped.

Aelsong said, "Great Paddy. The crap has hit the wind."

Ram looked at Song and Elora and said, "Stay here," forcefully enough to let both know he meant it. As she slid out of the booth right behind him to follow and cover his back, Elora wondered who in the world he thought he was talking to.

When Ram reached the middle of the room he was facing several perturbed-looking Fae, but he was also flanked by a recently cured vampire and three Black Swan knights, one of whom was a berserker and another of whom was his wife who could destroy the building if she had cause.

He said to the crowd in general. "We do no' want trouble. We are here on official business. If our presence makes you uncomfortable, we'll be leavin'."

One of the Fae staring down Ram smirked, raised his voice and said, "Hey, Duffy. The Fen is sayin' he's here on official business."

Aelsong's angel came through the crowd and stood in front of Ram. As she approached, she noticed he was as tall as her brother, which meant he was tall for a Fae. She stopped beside Ram in a show of solidarity.

The angel looked down at her. "You're with him, then?"

"For all eternity. He's my brother."

The prince's mouth turned up at the edges. Then he looked at Ram. "And what be the nature of your official business?"

"Again, we do no' want trouble and are willin' to leave, but why should we be tellin' you our business?"

One of the challengers pointed a thumb at Song's angel. "Are ye daft? You're talkin' to Prince Duff Torquil. You could be sayin' he's the last word on official."

Prince Torquil noticed that Ram showed no outward sign of being either intimidated or impressed.

Aelsong raised her chin and let her eyes wander over him again. A dark fae.

"'Tis no' for public consumption," Ram said.

"I see. And is your sister privy to this intrigue?"

"Aye."

"Very well. Have her come o'er here and whisper it in my ear."

"My sister is no' chattel. I do no' tell her what to do."

At that so very public statement of confidence, Aelsong's heart swelled with pride and affection. She looked at her brother with unconditional adoration for all of two seconds before she walked to the Scotia prince purposefully and stood on tiptoe to whisper, "Black Swan," in his ear.

Duff experienced a moment of sensory overload, a little light-headedness, when Song came near enough to kiss. He couldn't decide whether to focus on her very arousing scent which would have to be called Carnal Knowledge if it could be bottled, or the warmth of her breath on his ear, or the sound of her tinkling wind chimes voice, or the actual words she said. When he managed to restart his mental processes, it registered that she had mentioned The Order.

He looked down into those hypnotic Hawking blue eyes and said loud enough that everybody in the bar could hear, "The elves are in Scotia under my protection." Under his breath, quietly enough that only she could hear, he said, "Fae's gods, it can no' be."

Aelsong swallowed and looked up with wide eyes, her heart shaped mouth forming a silent "o". She started to take a step backward, but he grabbed her wrist. *"What's your name?"*

"Aelsong Hawking."

He looked like his future had just turned inside out and his brows drew together as he looked down at her. "Hawking?" His heart was sinking.

She backed up a couple of steps unable to look away then Duff's boisterous friends grabbed him and dragged him away.

EXCERPT II *The Witch's Dream*

They had allowed Aelsong to come since she was officially employed by The Order and was the inductee's sister. Only one other honoree was still living and, at eighty-seven, said he wouldn't have missed it. The royal family had sent the prince as their representative.

When they removed the silk draping from Ram's portrait, Elora didn't even try to stop big tears from rushing down her cheeks and falling on the wool sash of her dress uniform. He looked exactly as he had that Yuletide day she arrived at the cottage in New Forest with his hair pulled back behind his ears, in hunting costume, and his Black Watch Tartan gathered around his shoulders. The artist was as masterful as Rembrandt. The portrait, beautiful beyond description with mere words, but not nearly so beautiful as the elf himself. He beamed as she pressed her lips to his ear and told him there never had lived a male more glorious.

It hadn't escaped Elora's notice that Prince Duff Torquil and Princess Aelsong Hawking continually stole furtive glances at one another throughout the ceremony. She was hoping it had escaped the attention of everyone else.

As inductee, Ram was toasted with champagne and asked to personally speak to everyone in attendance. While he was busy, Elora saw an opportunity to have a word with the prince who was, in his own right, handsome as any fairytale ever imagined in his kilt which was probably his uniform for official state occasions.

She knew she might have only a couple of moments to talk without being overheard.

"Your Highness," she began, "I'm Elora Laiken, proud spouse of the honoree."

Up close she could see that the dark blue in his eyes was coupled with shades of violet. They were so unusual she may have stared just a second too long.

With a smile he said, "I well remember seein' you in the pub last night."

"Was that just last night?" She looked genuinely surprised and he laughed. "Is it difficult for

you being here to honor an elf?"

The prince's smile didn't falter, but he seemed to be trying to judge what she might be after. "No' at all, madam. Like many of my contemporaries, I believe 'tis time to put our differences aside. So far as I can tell, it serves no constructive purpose. In short, 'tis silly to continue for the sake of continuin'. But, if I see that in a headline on the morrow claimin' to quote me, I will deny it 'til the Highlands look level."

"I'm pleased to hear your progressive views on the subject. I vow your secret is safe with me though I must add that, if everyone keeps their more abrasive views secret, nothing ever changes."

The prince pursed his lips and nodded. "A good point and well said."

"These contemporaries who share your views were not with you at the pub."

"'Tis true. You caught me sneakin' out on my miscreant night." Elora had to laugh. "Boys from school who can be a little rough after a few pints."

The young prince had an engaging way about him. "It's been very nice to have this talk. I will try to get my husband to reexamine his position on the feud." The prince's lips twitched when she said the word feud. He was thinking that only an outsider could so minimize the past thousand years of elf and fae at war with each other. "And I will also work on *my esteemed brother-in-law from the inside."*

"Esteemed. A cautious compliment I would say." Torquil's eyes twinkled.

Elora laughed. "You've met him?"

The prince shook his head slightly. "Certainly no'. Let us say I have heard he is no'... a lot of laughs." They both shared a chuckle at the expense of the King of Ireland.

"Perhaps you could begin to ease your own reservations about the status quo into the discussion in your household as well?'

"'Tis a good plan and certainly I enjoy a conspiracy as much as the next prince, but my elders are no' showin' signs of bein' moved either in their political views or away from the throne. 'Twill likely be a long time fore I am king.

"If I may ask, though, what is your mate's position on this question?"

"He's never spelled it out as such, but, the night I first met him, he turned red in the face and turned over a chair at dinner because he thought I was calling him a fairy."

The prince looked serious. "Were you?"

She smiled. "It was an error of innocence. I come from a culture where everyone knows a collection of stories by the name fairytales. Something about that was mentioned."

"I see. And he was much offended."

Elora nodded. "Well, one step at a time then?"

"Always a sound policy."

"Meanwhile, do you think I can trust that my young sister-in-law will be safe in your country? She's the one over there who could almost challenge my husband for good looks."

The prince regarded her with amusement as if to say, "I know that you know and you know that I know. The question is does she know that you know what I know?"

"Fae's gods I pray 'tis so and 'tis no' said casually." He looked past Elora to where Aelsong was talking to guests and stealing glances at him. Sensing that Elora might prove to be a valuable and trusted ally, he leaned a little closer to her. "'Tis most unfortunate that I can no' see to it personally. Tragically so, as a matter of fact. One of the problems with your traditional approach to diplomatic relations is that diplomacy takes a very long time."

"Forgive me for saying that is a youthfully impatient remark, your Highness."

"Oh, aye," he laughed. "And how old be you, Madam?"

She patted her tummy and smiled. "Old enough to be someone's mother. Soon."

"Congratulations to you and the hero of the

hour."

"Of the millennium," she corrected.

"So. 'Tis a love match then." He grinned and cast a glance in Aelsong's direction without realizing he had paired the phrase 'love match' with a need to look her way.

At the same time, Elora saw that her conversation with the prince had drawn Ram's attention and that he was regarding her with distinct curiosity. Not wanting to press her luck, she said good night to Duff Torquil who stopped her long enough to shake her hand as he palmed off a card with his personal number on it. "Let us no' lose touch as the Americans say."

Elora walked away wondering where she could put that card. She thought about her bra and then laughed to herself. Had she seriously entertained the idea, even for a millisecond, that her bra might be a safe place to hide something from Ram? She walked straight to Kay and told him she needed him to keep something for her, no questions asked. As she knew he would, he pocketed the card looking straight ahead, no questions asked.

Gods. She loved Bad Company.

EXCERPT III *The Witch's Dream*

"Okay. Well, here's the thing then. We haven't had a chance to really get to know each other yet, but I grew up oldest of six. I had five sibs in my own world and two of them were girls. So I have experience being a big sis and I'm comfortable in the role."

"Oh. Aye." Song looked like she wondered where this was going.

"While we're gone for Kay's wedding, you'll be here completely on your own." Song nodded. "Away from home for the first time." She nodded again. "So, on that note, I'm volunteering to put my nose where it wasn't invited and offer advice. It will be best if you take every care to avoid Duffy for now."

Aelsong looked a little baffled, a little surprised, and a lot paler. "Duffy?" she asked cautiously.

"The Prince. You do know his name is Duff and his hooligan friends call him Duffy?"

Song nodded ever so slightly while her expression read shell-shocked. "How did you know?"

Elora pointed at her face with two fingers. "Eyes."

"We were so obvious?"

"Apparently not. Astonishing as it is, I seem to be the only one awake enough to see what is plain as day." Song blew out a breath of relief on learning that her brother was unaware. "I'm going to do everything in my power to help you, but it's going to take some time and a miracle or two."

She was looking at Elora with wide, hopeful eyes that could break Elora's heart. "People around here know how to make miracles. Right?"

Elora cocked her head while she appraised Aelsong. "Can you read for yourself?"

Song shook her head. "That would be handy, but my own future just whirls around like...sort of like smoke. If I try to force it, I see bad things - no' the actual future - things scary enough to make me stop askin'."

"And you can't ask anyone else in this department to read for you because of what they might see."

"Aye. Exactly."

"Well," Elora reached over and patted Song's hand, "when we get back I will start working on your mother and your brother. And your other brother. But it must be gradual. It's a big change we're hoping for. And Duff is going to see how far he can get from his side."

Song's lips parted and she hissed in a little air. "I saw you speak to him."

Elora smiled at her sister-in-law's reaction. "Guess what we talked about. Indirectly, of course."

Song's eyes coated with a dreamy expression.

"He was so gorgeous in his kilt, was he no'? It made my heart hurt."

Elora smiled, knowing exactly how it feels to find a male so beautiful you never want to look away. "Indeed. He is a real life Prince Charming."

Song looked confused. "You mean he's a charmin' prince?"

Elora sighed. She might never get used to living in a dimension without fairytales. "Right. Anyway. He says he has nothing personal against elves and thinks that continuing the feud is silly. That was his word. But he also said that, if I quoted him on that, he would be forced to deny it. He thinks there is a growing movement among some of his peers to resolve the dispute and put an end to the animosity."

Aelsong looked even more enraptured. "He said that?"

"Yes. That does not mean it will happen. He indicated that the mission is daunting from his side."

"Aye. 'Tis from mine to be certain."

"So we're agreed? You'll lay low while I'm gone?"

"Lay low?"

"It means be super discreet and prudent."

Song grinned. "I shall lay low like a rug."

Gaia kicked at the door lightly and they heard a muffled, "Hands full. Get the door."

Aelsong opened the door to let her roommate in.

Elora stood and readied herself to leave. *"Don't tell your brother I was here."*

"Alright then. Why no'?"

"Because, due to a turn of events that couldn't possibly be more ironic, I believe he thinks I'm a bad influence on you."

Song blinked twice before erupting into a toothy laugh that started in her belly and ended deep in her throat. Enough said. Elora got a quick hug goodbye and was gone.

EXCERPT IV *A Summoner's Tale*

"What do you know about my sister and that prancin' prick of a fairy prince?"

Elora blinked, but in the space of that flutter he learned all he needed to know. He had found out the first time Storm brought her to poker night, back at Jefferson Unit, that her very expressive face telegraphed even the tiniest nuance or feeling or thought. By now he knew her so well that she was as transparent as air.

She was caught off guard because she hadn't expected that question while Ram was cooking a leisurely Sunday breakfast. She recovered and tried to cover.

"Say that three times fast?"

"No' goin' to work this time. Stay on topic."

"You just don't like him because he can stand toe to toe with you and not be cowed by the H.O.H. elfster."

"ELFSTER!? What in Paddy's Name, Elora? And what is H.O.H.?"

"Hall of Heroes."

Ram turned away from frying bacon and gave her a look. It probably didn't have the effect he intended. He was wearing jeans, a long sleeve black tee that stretched across his chest enticingly, and a black Jack Daniels apron tied around his waist. She thought perhaps nothing was sexier than watching Ram's muscles ripple while cooking her breakfast.

"Do no' try to deflect. 'Tis I. And Paddy knows I can tell when you're hidin' somethin'." Ram looked determined.

Glen was giving Blackie a goodbye rough and tumble.

"Not in my living room," Elora said on her way past with her arms full of stuff the baby might *need on the plane. She set the load down by the front door, looked around nervously, and pulled Glen aside looking like a woman with conspiracy on her mind. She spoke in a tone that was barely above a whisper. "I need you to do something for me on the down low."*

"The down low?"

"Um. Yes. What do they call it here when you're off the record?"

"Off the record."

Elora let out a breath. "Okay. Off the record..."

"Which record are we off?"

"Let's start over. Between you and me..."

"Okay."

"Glen. Shut up." He chuckled. "You're messing with me, aren't you?" He grinned.

"Enough. Limited time here." He nodded.

"I need you to find out everything you can about the elf/fae war."

"Why?"

"Great Paddy, Glen."

"Okay. What exactly are you after?"

"How it started. See if you can find a reliable source - either a primary reference or an authority who knows for sure."

"You got it, boss."

"What has he got?" Ram came in carrying

another load of stuff the baby might need on the plane, wearing his damn extra-sensitive elf ears.

"Just getting Glen to keep an eye on my puppies. Like we talked about."

Ram nodded, opened the front door, and started carrying Helm's busload of necessities to the Range Rover.

"Scary," Glen whispered to Elora.

"What?"

"How easily you lied to him and how genuine it sounded."

"Yeah, well, keep that in mind if you ever get married."

"I'm starting to recognize the appeal of bachelorhood."

Elora pinned him with a look. "Seriously, I would never lie to him if it wasn't to protect someone."

"You're protecting somebody?"

"Yes. I'm protecting them. I'm protecting him. And I'm protecting them from him."

"I'll find out what you want to know."

Elora gave him her high beam smile. "You're the best."

"Is payment involved?"

"Yes. Here it is." She kissed him on the cheek just as Ram came back through the front door.

"Catch! Stop cruisin' my wife and help me move the entire inventory of Babes R Us to the armored tank."

EXCERPT V *Moonlight*

Prince Duff Torquil's family was having a small reception to celebrate his mid-winter graduation from law school from The University of Strathclyde at Glasgow. There was a tradition among the fae monarchy that those who were likely to rule should study history, with an emphasis on Fae history, and go on to law school, the logic being that the law was best administered by those who knew and understood it. The royal family, currently in residence at Holyrood Palace in Edinburgh, considered eight hundred guests a small reception. At that, there were sure to be at least two thousand more who would be in a snit and consider their lack of an invitation a snub.

When Elora received her invitation, she had written to the prince and explained that she and her husband had taken temporary quarters in the States. She added that she hoped it would not be presumptuous of her to ask that her good friend, Istvan Baka, and his bride, both employed by the same organization, take their place. Of course she knew it was presumptuous. After all, she had a background in the gentility of social arts, but she hoped he would grasp the code of her next sentence, which was this:

"You are certain to enjoy Baka's company and that of his new bride, who is popular among the entry level associates where she works. I'm certain you would make a loyal ally for life should you be kind enough to offer an extra invitation for her to bring a friend."

On the off chance that people were smarter than they appeared to be, Duff reread the note twice before tossing it on the glowing embers of the fireplace in his north wing office. He stabbed at the coals with the poker until the paper caught. After watching it burn to ash, he opened the door and stepped out to speak to his secretary. No matter how many times it occurred, the man always appeared startled when the prince leaned out and spoke to him. It seemed the palace staff would never get used to Duff's inappropriately modern and decidedly boorish behavior.

At first it had annoyed Duff that Grieve jumped in his chair whenever Duff opened the door to the outer offices and spoke to him. Grieve had been appointed by his father without giving the prince any say in the matter. Whatsoever. As usual. But eventually he came to terms with the fact that there was an odd little bespectacled man sitting just outside the entrance to his suite of rooms. He managed this internal resolution largely by appreciating the humor of the thing.

Grieve's display of shock had become part of Duff's day to day reality and one that he'd come to look forward to. In fact, he imagined that, should Grieve develop nerves of steel, he, Duff Torquil, Prince of the Scotia Fae and heir to the throne, would be forced to devise ways to deliberately create surprises, simply for the pleasure of seeing Grieve jump, gasp, and clutch his chest.

With that thought, Duff lowered his chin into his chest and chuckled while Grieve got himself together.

"Grieve," Duff repeated.

"Aye, your Highness."

"Please send an additional reception invitation to an Istvan Baka at the Black Swan Charitable Corporation offices, Charlotte Square."

"But, sir, there are no odd invitations left to offer."

"Are you goin'?"

Grieve pushed his glasses higher on his nose. "Oh, aye. My presence is expected."

Victoria Danann

"Do you want to go?"

Grieve hesitated, mouth open, while trying to decide whether it would be in his interest to speak plainly or not. "I, ah..."

"The truth, man."

"No' particularly."

"There you have it then. Problem solved." Duff ducked his head back into his rooms and began to close the door.

"But, sir, your father..."

The prince opened the door and reappeared, but without his customary affable and approachable expression. He was clearly not pleased and might even have been scowling, although it could be hard to tell on such a beautifully smooth and youthful face.

"Who do you work for, Grieve?"

"You, sir?"

"Is that a question or an answer?"

"An answer, sir?"

"Hmmm. Well. I understand that my father hired you."

"Aye, sir."

"But he is no' in a position to oversee the minutia of my affairs every day. Do you no' agree?"

Grieve nodded. "Aye, sir?"

"Well, then it seems you must make a choice. Is your loyalty to the one who appointed you or to the *one whom you serve?"*

Grieve paused for only a moment before standing and pulling his shoulders back. "My loyalty is to you, sir. You can rely on me."

Truly, Duff was half joking and had not expected the equivalent of a chivalric vow of service, but seeing that the little man was serious, the prince was touched and decided not to dismiss it as a jest.

"Thank you, Grieve. I will treasure your declaration and count on it, from this day forward."

Looking like he had just experienced the best moment of his life, Grieve smiled like he'd just been knighted.

Duff withdrew and closed the door, but stowed away in his heart the knowledge that allies could be made from something so small as a little respect and recognition.

Baka would have loved to skip the prince's reception, but Elora had asked him to go and take Aelsong. So he was standing in front of the bathroom mirror in a blindingly white pleated shirt, trying to tie his black tie. He was just glad his tux came with pants instead of the kilt that most of the male guests would be wearing beneath their formal jackets.

Fresh from the bath, Heaven came up behind

him with a towel wrapped around her. She pressed into his back and rose to her tip toes to peek over his shoulder at his reflection in the mirror.

"Hmmm. Handsome."

Baka gave her his best debonair smile. "Bond. James Bond."

She giggled. "Here." She urged him to turn around so that she could finish the tie. He could have used a clip-on, but the extra trouble paid off. While she was doing that, he casually unfastened her towel and let it drop to the floor. He pulled her closer with one hand while the other found delightfully wicked things to do to occupy itself.

Baka loved the way her chest heaved when she sucked in a surprised breath. "You don't really want this tied, do you, James?" Her voice had taken on a sultry undertone.

He laughed softly. "Not as much as I want to touch the valet. In fact..." Grabbing her waist, he lifted, turned and set her on the edge of the bathroom counter and stepped between her legs. "...what if we just...?" He froze in place when the door chime rang.

Heaven pushed him back and wiggled down from her perch making him groan as she slid down his body to the floor. "That's Song. Go get the door and entertain her for a few minutes while I finish getting ready."

He acquiesced with a big indulgent sigh and a look that was as good as a promise about what would take place when they were alone again later that night.

Baka pulled open the door and gestured for her to enter. "Song. You look lovely." His baritone had a velvety quality that made compliments sound smooth and sincere as vintage malt.

She hoped "lovely" was an understatement. She was going for good-as-it-gets and had pulled out all the stops.

"Thank you, Baka." She stepped in, looking him up and down. "No one would ever guess there's a dirty old vampire lurking underneath those pretty clothes. And I do mean old."

He chuckled good-naturedly. "My lurking days are over."

Nodding toward the bedroom, he added, "She's almost ready. I think. Something to drink while we wait?" He pointed to a bar that had been cleverly hidden in an antique French secretary.

"No. No' drinkin', breathin' nor sittin' down in this dress or 'twill crease and look a fright."

"Okay. We'll stand up together." The conversation dipped into a lag. "So. What's the mystery behind why the Lady Laiken wanted you to attend this party?"

Aelsong Hawking had the sort of expressive face that revealed every emotion, no matter how small, no matter how fleeting. That was doubly so when the observer was someone who had lived as long as Baka. She might choose not to tell him what it was about, but it was clear that something was up.

"Other than the fact that my sister-in-law seems to like seein' me happy, I do no' have a clue."

Baka knew she was lying. Aelsong knew that he knew she was lying, but he arched a brow and let it go. That was the best that could be expected.

The bedroom door opened and Heaven walked into the living room in very high heels and a shortened, tightened version of the blood-red dress she got married in. She was stunning. Stunning and delighted that Baka was speechless. His face said he liked this version of that dress even better. Her responding smile was like a starburst.

"Great Paddy, Heaven! You can no' go with me lookin' like that. 'Tis a crime for old married women to go sashayin' about the countryside drawin' all the attention for themselves. You should stay home with your old stodgy husband."

"Song. Those are the nicest things anybody's ever said to me. Thank you."

The "old stodgy husband" wasn't as pleased. "Well, it's not the nicest thing anybody's ever said to *me! I am the furthest thing from stodgy and you know it."*

Her gaze flew wide-eyed to Baka as soon as he said it, which alerted Heaven to the fact that there was something in that statement that alarmed Aelsong. Baka wasn't the only person who could read Song easily.

Song had learned enough about humans to know that Heaven would sever the friendship if she knew that Song had shared a memorable night with Baka, one that was wild even by elf standards, and she knew Heaven wouldn't care that it was before she'd met Baka. At least in that lifetime.

"What's going on?" Heaven looked directly at Baka. "What do you mean 'and you know it'?"

"Um. I met Aelsong in Ireland when Ram and Elora were getting married." True. "Didn't I tell you?" No. "I stayed drunk most of the weekend." Also true. "And I kept company with some of the attendees of feminine persuasion." True again, if somewhat understated and a masterfully executed dodge.

"Oh." Heaven looked uncertain, like the conversation had taken an unfortunate turn down a blind alley. She didn't know how to backtrack and recover the mood. Fortunately Baka did.

He gathered her in his arms with a devilishly intimate and reassuring grin. "You are absolutely the most ravishing, beguiling woman in this dimension or any other. And I haven't given another female a thought since the day Director Tvelgar introduced us."

The tension eased when she responded with a crooked little smile. "Introduced us? That's what we're calling it?"

"Works for me."

"Me, too." Song opened the door. "Let's get this party started. The royal family of Scotia awaits."

Baka stepped into the hallway and offered both arms to the lovely ladies on either side of him as the three dazzled their way toward the elevator.

The palace was an easy walk in walking shoes and a marathon in high heels. The doorman had a car and driver waiting, as promised. The women were having such a good time being dressed to kill that Baka was glad about going after all.

Aelsong insisted on an old-fashioned London-style cab so that she could half-stand in the car and try to keep from creasing her dress. "Just a warnin'. Tonight I'm along to listen, no' to talk. If I speak they'll know I'm elf and the ground might open up and swallow us all."

Heaven seemed to mull that over. "You mean the only difference between fae and elves is dialect?"

Song screwed up her face. "Can no' say for

sure. But 'tis a tip off. That I can say for sure. You will have to give me cover. Worse comin' to worse, just say I'm mute." When Heaven laughed, Song didn't like the impish look in her eye. "You would no'."

"Would not what?" Heaven batted her eyelashes and feigned innocence.

"You would no' deliberately say thin's, knowin' I can no' respond, that would make me either want to explode or want to squeeze your neck until that pretty amber necklace is permanently embedded!"

Baka was always surprised when reminded just how young his wife really was. "Come now. Nobody is choking anybody else. Heaven will behave."

Heaven looked out the window. "You can behave if you wish, stodgy old man. I will do what seems most fun at the time."

That threat miffed Song enough to make her forget about creasing the peau de soie dress. She sat unceremoniously and tried to reach over Baka to pinch Heaven. Baka blocked her with a stiff forearm while Heaven laughed with the impunity of a lady being protected by a powerful husband.

Baka stood on the fringe of the ballroom talking quietly with Simon Tvelgar. Both men were *more interested in using their evening to discuss business than to engage in painfully inane small talk, chatting up people they would probably not see again, if they were lucky. Baka actually saw it as a momentous opportunity, because Simon's hectic schedule left him pressed for time and difficult to see. It was a bit of a challenge to manage verbal code so that nothing said between them would seem extraordinary if overheard.*

Now and then Baka's eyes were drawn to his spouse's heavenly body moving through the room in her scarlet dress and her fuck-me shoes. So far as he was concerned all her shoes were fuck-me shoes, but the heels she wore that night screamed naughty by anybody's standards. There could be no doubt that she was having a marvelous time pulling the other beauty along, introducing Song to everyone as her very pretty, but tragically mute friend.

At one point Song leaned into Heaven with a big grin and spoke next to her ear without moving her lips. "I will get you for this if I have to spend years waitin' for the right moment."

Without looking at her companion, Heaven smiled and said, to no one in particular, but within Song's earshot, "Shaking in my knickers, darling. Oh, look, there's someone you haven't met." She grabbed Song to drag her in the direction pointed out by

Heaven's beautifully manicured and scandalously red fingernail.

Song gave her a look so evil it would curdle milk. "Years," was all she said.

Baka suspected Heaven was having fun at Song's expense, but it would have been impossible not to appreciate the essence of life and liveliness in that sort of youthful mischief.

Turning back to Simon, with one hand in his pants pocket, the other holding a heavy crystal tumbler of Scotch etched with the monarchy's coat of arms, Baka did look as if he could pass for James Bond.

"One thing is clear. It isn't going to be as easy as we had hoped. So far it's been Myrtle's Law regarding getting the Inversion kick-started. Everything that could go wrong has gone wrong."

"And you couldn't be more wrong about that," Simon replied.

"How so?"

"The worst thing that could have happened would be for the head of the task force to be reinfected with the virus, thereby becoming part of the problem instead of part of the solution."

Baka opened his mouth to respond, but his attention was redirected by a small fanfare.

The prince was being introduced and making

a grand entrance.

*Heaven leaned toward Song. "Do not tell my
husband I said this, but oh, my, my."*

*Duff's eyes found Song like heat-seeking
missiles. It was uncanny. Only a lifetime of pressure
cooker discipline enabled him to tear his gaze away.
But not before Heaven caught it. "Uh oh."*

*Song looked at Heaven and shook her head
with such a tiny movement that it would have been
missed by anyone not staring at her. That, coupled
with the pleading look in Song's eyes, told Heaven all
she needed to know.*

*"Let me take back that 'uh oh'." She glanced at
the prince. "Bloody buggin' bags full of shite is what I
should have said."*

*A guest standing nearby turned and gave
Heaven a look of censure to indicate her severe
disapproval of the word choice. Heaven just smiled
and bowed her head gracefully like she was a courtier
in a Renaissance play. The polite vocabulary enforcer
seemed to accept that and moved on.*

*Heaven turned back to ask Song what the
plaintive look was about, but she was gone. While
Heaven had been posturing for a stranger who needed
some business of her own to mind, Song had noticed
a little fae with glasses motioning her toward an
alcove. Excited by the intrigue and the idea of possibly*

speaking to the prince, she ducked off to the side. He placed a handwritten note in her hand surreptitiously.

Her heart was beating a little faster as she opened it and read the words, Meet me. -D. She experienced one of those rare, surreal moments when her intuition worked on herself. And she knew her life was going to be permanently divided into everything that had come before that moment and everything that happened after she'd read the note she was crushing in her gloved hand.

Concealing the note in the palm of her hand, she slipped it into her little bag then looked squarely into the face of the messenger.

"Come with me?" The verbal question mark at the end of that phrase left no doubt that it was not a command, but her choice. She nodded her assent. The time for considering was over. Her course had been set before she'd accepted the invitation to attend the prince's party.

Looking back over her shoulder to be sure no one was paying attention, she slipped away doing her best to look nonchalant and no one saw her leave. No one except a double ex vampire who had been asked to take her to the party and see to her safety while out and about in "fairyland". He had no intention of explaining to the Lady Laiken after the fact of whatever was afoot that he'd been too busy to pay attention to Song's comings and goings.

Baka set his glass on a sterling silver tray as it was carried past, excused himself from his conversation with Simon and followed Song with enough stealth to make a shadow envious.

Grieve led her down several deserted and dimly lit hallways, up a half tower of stairs then turned down a tiny curving hall that seemed to branch off and double back. He stopped next to another set of stairs leading higher.

"Down there." He pointed to the ground.

She stared at the stone steps beneath their feet. "Down where?"

"Fae Gods! You be elf!" he practically hissed.

She narrowed her eyes thinking it amazing that he had discerned that as the result of the utterance of two words. "Aye."

He stared for a moment, pressed his lips together, then shook his head. "Down. There!"

She looked closer at where he seemed to be pointing at the ground. At shin level there was an opening in the wall behind the steps. Her eyes jerked up at him. "'Tis a joke?" she hissed. "You can no' be serious! 'Tis your idea or his?"

"Have no fear, elf. You will fit. I assure you. I'm very good at spatial relationships."

"Spatial relationships," she repeated in a dry tone. "By that you would be meanin' the relationship between the flare of my hips and the width of that openin'."

He blushed a little and looked down, not meeting her eye. "Oh, aye."

"You're thinkin' I will be agreein' to acrobatics on a dusty stair? In this dress?" He continued to look at the ground, but said nothing more.

Song bent at the waist to take a closer look thinking that she could not believe she was considering it for even a millisecond. There did appear to be a room beyond the little opening, but it was too dark to make out what was in there. She looked at Grieve. "You'll be gettin' the dry cleanin' bill and 'twon't be cheap. I can promise you that."

With two fearless older brothers, Aelsong wasn't big on shrinking from challenges. She gripped her little beaded evening bag with her teeth so that she could hold onto the banister with both hands and lowered herself part way, feet first, before letting go. Her hips brushed against old stone steps as her lower body let gravity do most of the work.

She let go of the railing, expecting to drop, but squeaked in surprise when strong hands gripped her waist. She knew that scent. Duff Torquil. He chuckled, preening with male satisfaction as he slowly *lowered her down the front of his body. Aelsong, who was anything but inexperienced sexually, caught her breath and decided that, fully clothed and in the near dark, it was still easily the single most erotic moment of her life.*

There was just enough light in the room to see the extraordinary shine in the prince's eyes. Every cell of their bodies caught the fire of mating excitation as the ancient and mysterious magnetism did its work. He pulled her closer for a sweet and tender kiss that heated to flash boiling. Since neither of them had ever felt mating frenzy, they were both surprised by the intensity and immediacy of the passion.

Duff took hold of her shoulders and forced himself to break the kiss. Taking a step back, he managed to whisper, "H'lo beautiful," even though his breathing was uneven. "You came."

"No' yet." Ram's sister she simply couldn't let that opening slide.

She tore her eyes away long enough to look around. The room under the stairs was where the palace staff kept the royal family's collection of pewter plates, trays, goblets, tankards and pitchers. There was a large rectangular table in the middle of the room laden with gun-metal gray objects and every wall was lined with crowded shelves.

"Where are we?" she whispered.

He glanced around. "Pewter Room."

"How did you know about this?" She waved at the opening between the steps.

"I used to play hide and go seek with other kids whose parents worked here. I never lost and nobody ever figured it out. The hard part was stayin' in here by myself and bein' quiet until they gave up."

"Shows patience."

"Aye. I'm almost out where you're concerned."

They looked at each other in the semi-darkness for a few seconds before throwing themselves into kisses and clutches with renewed fervor. Independently, each was thinking they had never experienced anything in life half as good as the feel of each other and each was thinking they never wanted to stop or let go. Again, Duff pushed away.

"What are we goin' to do?" Song's whispered question was couched in between breaths that were coming fast. She was almost panting.

He reached out for one of her blonde curls and rubbed it between his fingers. His eyes met and searched hers. "Run away?"

She stared into his darkened eyes for a few seconds then grinned. "I will if you will."

He laughed softly. "Let's do and say we did no'."

She nodded enthusiastically while he gave her

a crooked little sexy grin. Her features went smooth and he knew the moment she became serious. "Are we kiddin'?"

He searched her face before moving to cup her cheeks in his hands. "I do no' have a better plan. I wish I did." He placed a tender kiss on her forehead and then jerked back. "Do you have a phone in that little purse of yours?" She looked down, opened the clasp, pulled out her phone and handed it to him.

He took it and started adding his contact. "This is a private number. My private number. The ID is 'Yam'." He pulled his own phone from the inner pocket of his jacket and handed it to her. "Give me yours. You can call me anytime, but I will only answer when I can. Do no' leave voice message or text. I will see that you called and call you back when I'm alone."

"YAM?"

He smiled. "You are mine."

Her lips moved as she repeated the words silently. She tore her gaze away from his handsome face long enough to enter her number in his phone.

He looked at the contact. "IAY?"

"Aye. I am yours."

Duff opened his mouth to say something, but heard Grieve's hushed voice above their heads. "Sir. Someone's comin'."

Duff grabbed Song and kissed her like he thought he had one minute to live then, placing his forehead against hers, he said one word. "Soon."

He left through the room's actual door on the other side from where she'd dropped in. She heard Grieve speaking to someone above her head and knew she needed to remain as quiet and still as possible. Still feeling the warmth and tingle of his kiss on her mouth, she pressed her lips together and closed her eyes. Her mind was racing, imagining a hundred different scenarios of the future. The only thing they all had in common was a big comfy bed with a big and naked dark fae prince in it. Soon.

She smiled into the shadow-filled room, partly because of the idea of a lifetime with Duff Torquil and partly because it occurred to her that she might actually beat her older brother out of the position of family black sheep. Running off with a fae? She could see her father's face turning reddish-purple. She could see her mother's face pinched with disappointment and worry while hurrying away to oversee composition of a press release. Both her brothers would be turning the air blue enough to change the tint of the sky before vowing to hunt Duff down and skewer him.

At least she wasn't the heir. As difficult as it would be for her, she couldn't begin to imagine what

Duff would be up against with his family. She let out a whispered laugh. She never asked to be mated to a fae, but there was no point trying to deny it. Life was strange.

EXCERPT VI *Gathering Storm*
(conversation between Elora and Glen)

"You remember that thing you were doing for me. What I asked before we left Ireland?"

"You thought I forgot."

"Well…"

"Of course you would think that. I should have let you know I'm on it. It's a worthy mystery, tough enough to be fun, cool enough to be interesting. I was at the latest in a series of dead ends, but I've got a new lead. So the trail is heating up again. As soon as Sol gets back I'll request some time off and a pass ride."

"Good news."

"I don't know yet."

"Well, I'm hoping. I wish I could tell you why I need the intel so badly, but just to reiterate, it's important to some people I know. Really, really, really important."

Glen cocked his head. "Abandon-my-post

important? Or work-on-it-when-I-can important?"

"Scale of one to ten. One means if we never find out it's no big deal. Ten is the end of days. I'm putting this between seven and eight."

"Okay. You know I don't have any free time while Sol's gone and not much when he's here. And the lead I need to follow requires travel with flex time and a long leash."

"When Sol gets back, let me know what you need and I'll make it happen."

A TALE OF TWO KINGDOMS

We've called them by hundreds of different names.
At times they've shown themselves to us as they
are.
At times they've shown themselves in disguise.
We've used each other.

We've amused them, entertained them,
and provided breaks in their boredom.
In return, they've given us the illusion of reason or
inspiration or purpose or excuse.

CREATION

In an exercise as old as the stars, the divinity class teacher told his charges to divide into teams of eight so that he might assign group projects. As it happened there were eighty-seven in the class. Eighty of those responded with the excitement that would be expected from an opportunity to work in committee structure with their friends. They chatted animatedly, drawn to each other as if they were made of magnets. Appearing to be in a state of delight nearing euphoria, they began naming their teams and composing team cheers while they awaited further instructions.

Beneath the commotion, inaudible but nonetheless present, were the groans and anxious stomach rumbles of the remaining seven who would rather take a millennium's detention than participate in a group project. When the huddles were completely formed, those seven looked around to see who was left and gradually, grudgingly, began to drift toward one another.

Dr. Pierce quietly observed, looking down from a raised platform and a condescending attitude. He knew the process of group project assignation was painful for the socially vulnerable, but it wouldn't do for him to recognize that he enjoyed that. No, indeed. He viewed it with clinical dispassion, thinking it almost resembled a dance. Some were adept and some were not.

He was one of the first beings ever created and looked it. Though he had managed eternal survival physically, he'd discovered the truth of the Peter Principle rather early in his career and had, thereafter, become known for his bitterness expressed at times in biting wit and often misdirected at powerless students.

He watched the progress of the formation of the eleventh, odd number group, with some distaste. He resented the fact that his instructions were being delayed by the slowness with which they came together. He resented the fact that they were such ne'er-do-well loser misfits that they had forced him, in his own mind, to have already given them a failing grade on the project before they had even heard the assignment. Because of that he was already formulating a plan to give them the subject with the least likely chance of succeeding - the realms of Earth.

It wasn't intended as a punishment. Exactly. It was more an anti-reward.

The seven sat down at a corner conference table, eyeing each other cautiously, waiting to hear sentence pronounced – that being how long they would be stuck working together on a group project. None of them knew each other well enough to be labeled so much as acquaintances. Of course they'd seen each other around, but had never had either occasion or desire to interact on any level.

Still young and inexperienced in the grander scheme of things, they were aeons old, a concept unimaginable by lesser minds. They were a motley crew, beautiful for their oddities, pure in their extremes, comical in their eccentricities, but all of that could only be appreciated if viewed through a prism of generosity. And the absence of that was one of the essentials that had held Dr. Pierce back from a more illustrious and transcendent career.

Pierce restored quiet to the space by holding up his hands in a gesture of authority that was a tad grander than required for the event, but the preferred pupils were wily about their surreptitious jests at his expense. Pierce's assistant passed out the parameters of the assignment.

Every team would be given a world with a starter complement of elementals, flora, fauna... the usual. The common Hominin prototype was to be used to populate at least a portion of the dimensions. The more humans, the greater the points. The experiment would be judged as a whole, but each student would be encouraged to pursue an individual "hobby" project, which could result in extra credit.

As the students looked over the outline of the assignment, Dr. Pierce drifted down from his platform, holding eleven tablets. Each tablet held the name of the team's destination where they would be spending the next several thousand years together.

He drifted from one team to the next handing out tablets until there was only one tablet left and one team left, the team of seven, joined together by necessity rather than choice. One of them stood to receive the tablet and the others raised no objection. Pierce put it in his hand, then said to the group, "There are lessons to be learned from those who will people your study. When you have absorbed those lessons, you will return and advance to new challenges."

One of the seven said, "Oh, joy," sarcastically.

Pierce's gaze jerked toward him in reprimand. "Clearly that won't be soon. All the better for me."

When Pierce was gone, the one holding the tablet raised it and read it out loud. "Earth."

The seven looked at each other quizzically and responded with shaking heads and shrugging shoulders.

And so The Council was formed. The seven were...

Culain
Etana
Rager
Heralda the Dark

Ming Xia
Theasophie
Huber Quizno

CHAPTER 1

"Have you no' had a niggle of a tap then?"

Duff looked up at his friend. He'd been staring into a pool of dark ale like he was a soothsayer and it was a diviner's tool. They sat in a corner of a pub like a sad pair of leftover bachelors.

"Ah, Brean, no' you, too."

"Me, too? 'Tis only I here, Duffy. How many are you seein', man? And 'tis only your third pint."

"Was referrin' to me mum. Earlier this very e'en, was mindin' my own affairs when the grand dame comes sashayin' 'round and orders my own secretary away so that she can discreetly inquire as to my ability to mate."

Brean waited for two entire breaths before he began to beat the table and laugh hard enough to squeeze moisture from his eyes.

From a certain point of view, Duff supposed he could admit it might be comical.

Duff's mum had wandered into his suite that afternoon and nodded at Grieve in that way that said, "Did you no' just remember somethin' needs doin' down the hall there?"

As the door was open to his assistant's office, he was able to observe the entire exchange. Grieve,

who had not survived fifteen years in palace employ
without skills, knew how to take a subtle hint. He
rose, gave a slight bow, and asked for leave by excuse
of errand for the prince. She graciously gave him
leave.

Once the secretary had vacated the rooms, the
queen began to slowly walk about Grieve's office
looking at this, studying that, as if she was visiting a
museum and expecting to be tested later on what she
saw. She was exactly twenty-five years older than her
son and still lovely enough to drive sales of
magazines when she appeared on the cover.

He had gotten his big-boned frame and height
from his father, but his dark hair and violet eyes were
the unmistakable stamp of maternal genes.

"Social call, Mum?"

"What else, love?"

"Well, that's nice." Duff looked up. "Tea?"

"Thank you, no. Had my fill already."

There was nothing to do but wait until she
said what she had to say. "Would you care to sit
then?"

"Um? Aye, perhaps." She strutted herself to
the smart red leather armchair in front of Duff's desk
and sat down as gracefully as a woman half her age.
"I was thinkin'…" Duff groaned. "What was that?"

"Did no' say a thin', Mum."

Lorna Torquil was Queen of Scotia fae, but
for the moment, she was simply a woman looking at
the male child she had raised to adulthood, who was
also her own heart walking outside her body. He was
her only son, but he was also her only child, which
probably intensified her feelings. All that maternal

impulse was trained on one fae who normally saw that as a blessing.

"I was thinkin'," she began again, "that 'tis past time for the matin' to come callin'?"

The way she cocked her head he felt like he'd been placed on a glass rectangle and slid underneath a giant microscope for closer scrutiny.

"The matin'?"

"Aye. I look at the social pages, you know. I see how many of your friends have had you standin' up for them at their handfastin's. Droppin' all 'round you, are they no'?"

Her gaze was boring down. She was doing that mother thing. The one where she examined him closely, looking for some sign that he might be clipping the truth. It was some mystical means of lie detection that was practically foolproof.

He knew the color was spreading up his neck and he knew she could see it. So he decided the best cover was to laugh.

"Mum. You're embarrassin' me. Aye. I'm practically the last one standin'. Thanks very much for stoppin' by to point that out. Now I really ought to get 'round a couple details before…"

She stood abruptly. "Very well. I shall no' detain you from your *very* important work. Let me just leave you with the thought that you're no' likely to come face to face with your intended while you're shut up in here with Grieve. Because one thin' I'm certain of, she ain't him."

He laughed. "I can no' believe *you* said 'ain't'."

"Got your attention, did it?"

"You always have my attention."

"What a lovely liar you are, my love." She turned to go.

"Like your hair that way, Mum."

"Shut it," she said without turning back.

"And that would be 'she ain't he', no' 'she ain't him.'" he yelled after her and heard the muted tones of the bawdy laugh she reserved for when she was at home with family. She was already at the end of the long polished hallway, moving quickly with the resumed purpose of a woman who has a royal schedule to keep.

It had been over a year since Duff had first seen Aelsong Hawking sitting with her back to him in a pub in the shadow of the Balmoral Hotel. Since then he'd only seen her twice and, of those three encounters, had only been alone with her once.

He'd given Elora Laiken a chance to talk to her hothead husband and get him to lay some groundwork, or whatever her plan had been. He'd given the times a chance to change and, while some of the younger fae were definitely making noises that they didn't really see the point of the hostilities, there was no catalyst. No motivation sufficient enough for either side to move off dead center. There wasn't even a reason to talk about it.

The following day Duff had a mid-morning appointment with the Director of Communications. On the way back into his office he stopped to spin the giant globe that sat between the window and fireplace in the outer office occupied by Grieve. It was one of those objects that regularly failed to capture notice because of the combination of its familiarity and lack of use. On that particular day, however, something about the blues, greens, and yellows was captivating.

As the sphere rotated deosil, his eye was naturally drawn to Scotia, sitting atop the islands of Britannia to the north. Looking down at the top of the world, from his vantage point, he watched as the tundra of the cossacklands seemed to go on forever before coming to a small break where the Bering Sea separated continents. As rotation continued, he was reminded again of how drastically a flat map distorted the representation of size and space relationships on the Earth's surface and that Canada's land mass was immense.

As he was thinking just that, he reached out and stopped the globe with his large fingers under the word 'Canada'. His eyes moved to the right. He knew that people often talked about the severe Canadian cold, but Edinburgh, the city in which he was standing, was further north than every major Canadian city. Cold was not a Scotia fae's biggest problem.

He spoke to Grieve without turning around, allowing his eyes to continue to move over the uppermost band of North America: Newfoundland, Quebec, Ontario.

"Grieve."

"Sir."

"What do I have for the rest of the day?"

"Lunch at the Ministry of Finance. The king said to mark that one mandatory. The Royal Mile Tourist Commission will be here at three to petition you for permissions to use various national monuments for the stagin' of events."

"Hmmm."

"Photographs with royal scholarship recipients at four."

"How long will that take?" Grieve blinked as if he didn't fully grasp the question. "Without the usual dawdlin'."

"Without dawdlin', perhaps fifteen minutes."

"So done at four-fifteen then?"

"Aye."

"Call Pey and tell him I need to see him today. In a professional capacity. My office. His office. Dinner. I do no' care. Tell him I'm buyin' and tell him I'll no' be takin' no for an answer."

"May I ask how long an appointment you'll be requirin', your Highness?"

"I need a half hour for business, but would linger over dinner with port and cigars after if he has time. If 'tis to be dinner, reserve my table in the wine cellar at the club where we could talk without bein' overheard. Oh, and, Grieve…"

"Aye, your Highness?"

"Ah, never mind."

A couple of minutes later Grieve knocked lightly on Duff's office door and poked his head in.

"Mr. Innes says he can get a mutton quickie past his mate if 'tis early enough, but 'twill be safer to forego port for a better excuse. Yule perhaps."

Duff chuckled. "Tell him six then. Call the kitchen at Highlander and have them to do up a mutton saddle with roasted potatoes for the pair of us and have it ready to serve at six fifteen."

"Very good, sir."

CHAPTER 2

Glen closed the phone as Rosie opened the door of his office and strolled in smiling. She was wearing a backpack over her shoulder that was girlie-looking, made out of something like bronze satin, kind of vintage, kind of cute. Everything about Rosie was kind of cute except her nymphomania. And that was definitely hot.

"You ready?"

He looked at his watch. Three o'clock. Right on time. "Aye, my darlin'," Glen said with his very best attempt at an Irish lilt. Rosie laughed and nodded toward the door in a gesture of, "Let's go."

Glen had promised Elora he'd get to the bottom of the cause of the Elf Fae War four months before. He didn't like making excuses about the delay, but a few things had come up: Animal House, filling in for Sol, a major search and rescue operation for the real Storm with simultaneous makeover for a Storm pretender, Rosie... well, Rosie, aliens trying to demolish Jefferson Unit on his watch, and Sol dying having left him in charge and without naming a real replacement. *Criminently!*

A lesser person might have succumbed to a nervous breakdown, but he, the Great Glen, had managed to manage. More importantly, he emerged with the best lead so far. He'd promised Elora that he would pursue it as soon as he could get away for a week or so. Now the week was at hand. Jefferson was put back together. The people who had converged on J.U. from every corner of the globe to pay their respects to Sol had all returned to their respective stations of duty and things were quiet.

He was going to get away for a few days with his girl and do the Lady Laiken the favor of a secret mission at the same time. Of course it didn't hurt that his girl was first class transportation personified. Just the sort of companion needed for an impossible journey such as the one on which they were about to embark.

He had a very fine evening planned beginning with a ride through the passes, courtesy of his very lovely date, to Doolin, Ireland, where they would eat pub food at Gussie O'Connor's until they were ready to burst at the seams, see how many pipes and fiddles could cram into one pub on a fine Irish night, then snuggle together in a warm bed at Mrs. McGann's, thousands of miles away from where either of them was expected to be. Perfect.

Everything about Glen's first night in Ireland with Rosie was as wonderful as each of them had hoped it would be.

When they woke on their first morning after having slept together, Glen found out that there were a lot of unusual aspects to having a girlfriend like Rosie. He snuggled close to give her a morning kiss.

She turned her head and said, "Ew. No. Morning breath."

He said, "I don't care," and started to gather her close when she simply disappeared out of his arms. "Hey! No fair!"

He heard her giggle in the bath when the water came on. They were lucky to get a room with a bath. He threw back the covers and stood up, intending to stomp after her and show her who was boss, but was stifled by a gasp. The shock of the cold air in the room momentarily froze him in place. He looked down and realized that his privates had shriveled to miniature replicas of themselves and decided that he'd rather not present himself to Rosie in that condition after all.

She opened the bathroom door and looked at him with a question on her face.

"Cold," was all he could offer.

She laughed at him. "Get in the bed, big baby. I know how to fix that." Gently pushing him back under the covers, she eased her body on top of him. "You *are* cold."

He was shivering and his teeth were chattering.

"How can you possibly be so warm?"

As she began moving her body back and forth over his, creating the most delicious friction, she kissed the hollow of his throat, raised up and gave him a smile that was erotic and evil at the same time. "Maybe I have hellfire and brimstone in my veins, just like the Dante myths."

The light that originated behind his eyes was trained on her like a beam and made her catch her breath. She was sure that what she was seeing was what love looked like.

"Maybe, but it feels like heaven. So I don't care. Just keep doing that."

As he slid his ice cold hands over the cheeks

of her exquisitely curved derriere she jumped straight up with an, "Eek!"

He laughed, grabbed her around the middle with both arms and rolled her onto her back. "You got something for me?"

"Thanks to your magical womanly warming techniques, I *do* have something for you. You want it?"

She grinned. "Only if you can manage with no hands."

"No hands, huh?"

"Let me see what I can do about that."

The people in the room next door, who would have liked to sleep for another hour, might venture to say that Glen was a capable companion with or without hands. At least from the sound of things.

The cliffs were so windy Glen was afraid Rosie was going to blow right off. He supposed she could manage even if that did happen, but he was having to consciously work to stay upright.

He thought she was a good sport to agree to combine an investigation with a getaway. Of course there was always a chance that his lead was another dead end, in which case he would have to say that the only thing he had to show for his trouble was a fine few days with his sweet Rosie and some very happy balls. Though he would certainly omit the last of that when he reported to Rosie's auntie, the Lady Laiken.

The weather had turned cooler than normal and they had rummaged through the backpacks to layer clothes. The plan was for Rosie to transport herself out to the distant island, barely visible in the mists, so that she could spot the entrance to the fabled Ogram's cave where the hermit was purported to live. If she could find it, she would return for Glen and they would go together.

It was a plan custom designed to deflate a young man's ego, but it was also the most practical so Glen had to agree that sense trumped pride.

"Back in a flash."

She gave him a big kiss on the cheek and was gone. It only took Rosie a second to locate two shadows that could be possible targets. The first was only a shadow. The second was a cave, but only three feet deep. However, once at the entrance to that cave, it was possible to see another that was entirely obscured by a limestone lip that curved downward from a shelf above. It matched the description Glen gave her. She switched on the light, did a quick sweep, and went back for Glen knowing he'd be anxious.

He jumped when she materialized next to him, but at least didn't yelp. Thankfully.

She looked serious and started to shake her head.

His shoulders slumped a little. "Okay, well, it's just…"

She grinned. "It's there. Come on."

"What?"

He didn't have time to switch gears before he was standing inside the head of the cave.

"This is it, right?"

He couldn't see Rosie's face because the light was to her back.

"I think so."

He fumbled in his pack, retrieved a contraption with duct tape sticking out everywhere, and secured it to his head. Rosie was fascinated and hadn't yet decided whether she was going to laugh or worry.

"What is that?"

Glen made an adjustment on his forehead and then switched the thing on. The cave was flooded with light. "Oh. I didn't like any of the 'head lights'," he used air quotes, "on the market. This gives us a good six hours. It's a bike light. Nice, huh? A NiteRider 350, and a… um, jock strap. Look at that."

She smiled to herself, thinking it was hard to argue with results. "So what now?"

"Well, I guess we go further in? See if we can find the…"

"Hermit."

"Yeah. The hermit."

"You think there really is a hermit?"

"Well, the thing was right about the cave."

"The thing?"

He waved the paper in his hand. As they moved deeper into the cave the light from the entrance faded away as did the sounds of both wind and North Atlantic waves crashing into the cliff sides below. "Got a copy right here from Puddephatt. Claims the foremost authority on the subject of elf/fae history is this cave-dwelling hermit. Oral tradition."

"Oral tradition," she said drily. "Yes, but Glen. How would this hermit get in and out? What does he do for supplies? It would take hours to scale the cliffs and be almost impossible to do alone.

Unless you think he has a part Elemental delivery service?"

Glen stopped and, when he turned to face her, she squinted when the light shone straight in her eyes.

"Oops. Sorry." He pushed the light to the side so that he could face her without blinding her. "Why did you assume he's human? Maybe he's like you."

She looked around and raised her eyebrows. "Then why would he live here? It's bloody cold. You know? Did you bring hand warmers?"

"No. Here." He blew on her fingers while he was considering why anyone would live there. "I don't know why anybody would want to be a hermit much less why one would want to live in a cold cave." He stopped and held up a hand. "Shhhh."

They heard something like a pebble falling followed by a deep, but pleasant voice that sounded unmistakably amused. "Cause I like it here." Glen's head jerked in the direction of the sound and the light found the figure of an attractive elf who appeared fortyish, wearing jeans, a black tee, and biker boots. He was showing a couple days growth of blonde beard and his light curls were pulled back behind his ears. "You wantin' to see me?"

Glen felt Rosie crowd close against his back. "Ah. We did. Um. Do. If that's okay. If you're the, ah, hermit?"

The elf rubbed a hand over his scratchy face and smiled. "Hermit, is it?"

"We must be in the wrong place."

"Who sent ye?"

"Puddephatt."

"Bugger."

"We'll just be going."

"So I'm thinkin' you two are no' only young, but naive as well."

"Pardon?"

"Why are you thinkin' men become hermits?"

Rosie poked her head around Glen's shoulder. "Because they don't like people."

"Aye. So, that bein' the case, what were you thinkin' would be in store if you went callin' uninvited on someone who's an introvert to the third power? Tea and crumpets?"

"I'd like some," Rosie said.

"He's not offering, Rosie. He's being facetious," Glen said without taking his eyes off the elf.

"Still sounds good. I could use a hot tea." She shivered visibly.

The elf's mouth might have twitched just a little. "Well, had ye thought it through? What was your plan? And, for that matter, why are ye here?"

"Look. We're not spelunkers and we don't work for "I Wanna Know". We're here on an important errand for information that, apparently, only *you* have." Glen could feel Rosie shivering more against his back. The hermit was wearing a short sleeved shirt while appearing as warm as if he was in the tropics. "I guess it's part of the hermit job description to be rude so as to discourage guests."

"Guests?" He cocked an eyebrow. "That's what you're thinkin'?" He tried to peer around Glen to see Rosie better. "So what have you there behind you, young inquisitor?"

Glen scowled at the question and was just

about to tell Rosie to get them out of there. "Seriously, we…"

"Name's Finrar. Now you're here, you may as well get what you came for. Follow me."

He turned and walked away, leaving Glen wondering whether they should stay or go.

"Rosie, what do you think?"

Squeezed against his back, he felt her life her shoulder and drop it. "We can just go, pfffft pffffft if we don't like the direction of things."

"Okay. I like the way you think, but stay close because only you can go pfffft pfffft."

Soon the uneven rocky floor of the cave opened up to a flat sandy tunnel. They entered a light-filled chamber that was warm and comfortable.

The elf motioned for them to sit on a smooth limestone ledge. "Underground hot springs."

Rosie looked around. "Do you scale the cliffs every time you need food or supplies?"

The elf looked her up and down then waved his hand in the air. "There's another way in."

"Oh?"

"Hmmm. Tunnel access by a door in the side of a hillen. 'Tis well-concealed."

"Oh."

He smiled. "Does no' sound as glamorous or dangerous as a hermit scalin' the cliffs with meager stores for his inhospitable seaside cave?"

"Well, no. It doesn't."

"Exactly right."

"I see."

"So tell me why that old rat catcher sent you

'round here?"

Glen cleared his throat. "I'm on an errand for a knight of The Order of the Black Swan. Puddephatt said for me to tell you that." Finrar licked his bottom lip and nodded. "I'm to learn why the elves and fae are at war. No one seems to know. Every time I think I'm headed in the direction of a promising theory, it proves misleading. Puddephatt says that, if anyone knows, it's you."

The elf's eyes flicked to Rosie.

"I'm Glendennon Catch, by the way. I work for The Order. This is Rosie Storm. Her dad is a knight emeritus. Her mom is still on the payroll. Magick."

"Well, Rosie. I do no' have crumpets, but I could fire a pot of tea. As to you, Catch, what I have to give ye is the tale of how the Great War came to be. I can no' say 'tis fact. I can only say that, like most thin's called historical, 'tis a good measure of truth to be found within. If ye will have what I offer, I will give it."

"The words life and death were not used to describe the importance of my mission, but it was impressed upon me that the outcome is urgent. There's no doubt in my mind that the Lady Laiken needs us to return with anything we can learn. Whatever you have is treasure."

"Aye. Well, my experience with knights of The Order is that they have a leanin' towards the drama, as you may have noticed yourselves."

Glen's mouth fell open and he started to rise up in defense of all Black Swan knights, but Rosie grasped him by the arm with both hands and kept him sitting.

Victoria Danann

CHAPTER 3

In a short time, Finrar brought her tea made from leaves in a cup that appeared to be old hammered pewter. He handed her a small cloth to use for grasping the handle so she wouldn't burn herself and took a seat across from them.

"Does no' take long to tell 'cause very little of the detail is still known. 'Twas a long time ago. There were annals o'course, but nothin' remains of them.

"Have you ever heard of the Danu?"

Glen looked at Rosie. She shook her head. Glen turned back to Finrar and shook his head no.

"The children of Danu had migrated to this world and set up a colony in what is now the north of Wales. The country was rough and tumble, but that suited the Dana fine. They liked roasted meat and liquid spirits and they were right handy with song and dance, but they could also be a fierce bunch and were ready to fight at the blink of an eye.

"There was a place of witches in the Britons in those days. You might even say it was an Order. Some of those witches took a likin' to the Dana, thought we were magical or some such." He gave Rosie his boyish smile, so fetching, as if to say he knew full well why those witches thought they were magical. He was making a halfhearted attempt at pretending humility for courtesy's sake.

"When stories about Romans began to reach the western lands, the Dana paid no mind. Enemies are a fact of life like bugs and the occasional limp cock, so I hear, but the witches were alarmed and kept insistin' that the Romans were a great plague runnin' deep and wide. After a time they convinced the Dana to move the colony to an island in the middle of the Irish Sea where the witches could keep them safe. Once there, the ladies brought up a mist to shield the island from discovery.

"As the story goes, the mist provided an ideal hidin' place for creatures such as Dana and practices such as sorcery. But it also formed a sort of shield against inclement weather, like a sort of insular dome, good for growin' all manner of food, particularly apples.

"The Dana made good use of their time there. They learned Anglish." He smiled. "Even if they put their own stamp on it by retainin' the cadence of the old language. They shared their games and festivals and sacred observances with the witches, and the witches taught the females healin' and sight . Life was simple, quiet, and good.

"Within a few years the chief's mate bore twin sons. Twins were unheard of among the children of Danu, but no one thought anythin' of it except to see it as twice blessed.

"The boys, princes, were named Galfine and Galfae. Beautiful as the sun with eyes the color of the sea and hair shot through with streaks of rust and copper. They got on well with the other young ones and were everythin' the royal pair could ever have wished for.

"All was well until the boys were in the late part of their twenty-fourth year. They were struck by the matin' instinct at the same time. Now, normally, 'tis an occasion for rejoicin', but…"

"It was a woman," Glen said. "It's always a woman."

"Oh, what rot!" Rosie countered. "Shut up and let him finish the story."

"As I was sayin', and it sounds like you're both ahead of me, naturally the boys were both drawn to the same female. The new way of sayin' it is that they both originated from the same egg that split in two. The old way of sayin' it was that they were of the same heart and mind."

"What did the girl do?"

"Ah, the young female. Garineen. A tragic victim is what she was, susceptible to the same matin' impulse as the princes. She loved the both, no' one more than the other and could no' choose between them. It was breakin' her heart to see them fallin' out on her account. Thinkin' she could stop the feud by removin' herself from the equation, she had one o' the witches cast a spell to disguise her so that she would be invisible to them.

"I would like to tell you that the story ended there, with the ruin of three lives, but sadly that was no' the way of it. When the lads deduced that the object of their affection had been hidden by magical means and could no' be found, well… I was told that they were so enraged that their fury made the seas boil and the earth tremble, but I suspect that part was poetic embellishment.

"The brothers regarded each other with a hatred so complete they could no' tolerate the idea of occupyin' the same land mass. 'Twas at that point the children of Danu split into factions. Some sailed to the west with Galfine and claimed Ireland for their own. Some sailed to the east with Galfae and claimed Scotia for their own. A few stayed on the island of the witches, but no' many.

"The fin, or elves, of Ireland taught their children to despise the fae of Scotia and t'other way 'round. Generations went on, separated by the sea and no desire for contact. The speech gradually became different enough so that the Dana could identify one another as elf or fae on hearin' the tongue spoken. No doubt both clans are of a mind to believe the differences run deeper than a turn of syllable, but 'tis all there is to it.

Glen and Rosie sat for a couple of minutes in silence as if they were waiting for Finrar to say something else. Finally, Glen cleared his throat and asked, "Why do you think more people don't question the status quo?"

"Because the thin' about comfort zones is they're comfortable. 'Tis as much philosophy as may be expected from an introverted cave dweller such as myself."

Glen understood the cue and stood to leave. "It's way more than I expected to tell you the truth. We thank you very much for your time and for the information. It was, in fact, exactly what we needed."

"Yes," Rosie said. "Thank you for the tea.

And you have a lovely, um, environment."

Finrar smiled. "Shall I show you out then?"

"No. No," Glen said. "We know the way."

"Well, then."

"Yep. Going right now. The way we came. Won't tell a soul we've been here."

After a minute the echo of footsteps had faded into silence.

"You can come out now."

Deliverance emerged from the shadows. "You know what rhymes with introvert?" Finrar said nothing. "Pervert."

"Certainly you would know."

"So what's the game, Archie?"

"Don't call me that, demon." Kellareal resumed his innate form. "You know I'm not an archangel."

"Sensitive. Again, what are you playing at?"

"It's no game. It's Council business, which means it's none of yours."

"Maybe not, but my granddaughter *is* my business."

"I'm not going to hurt her and you know it."

"All the same, it won't hurt for you to know I'm watching."

The angel sighed. "If you must know, we're setting the wheels in motion to resolve this elf fae conflict."

"We?"

"They. The Council."

Deliverance gaped. "Excuse me while I fall

down laughing. The seven of them couldn't agree on a movie, much less resolve a two-thousand-year-old war. Fairies and pixies sharing a Coke?" He was shaking his head when he said, "Not in this dimension."

"There's no justification for ethnic slurs. They're stuck. They need a push."

The demon considered that. "A push, huh. What do you have in mind?"

Kellareal regarded him coolly. "Again. Not. Your. Business."

"Maybe I could help."

"When did you become interested in helping anyone other than yourself?"

The angel thought he may have seen just the briefest flicker of something other than jest or cynicism pass over Deliverance's flawless features, but he recovered so fast it was impossible to tell.

"I didn't. I'm not. Goodbye." And he was gone.

Rosie popped them back to their room and sat down on the edge of the bed. She looked up at Glen.

"If you knew how you looked with that thing on your head, I feel sure you would want to take it off."

Glen eyes drifted upward almost like he'd forgot he was wearing a biker light attached to his skull by a jockstrap. Actually he hadn't thought about it the entire time they'd been with Finrar. Pulling the contraption off his head, he looked at it like he'd never seen it before and was embarrassed for himself in arrears.

"Why didn't you tell me?"

Rosie laughed. "I didn't think about it either." She saw that he was serious. "What's the matter, Glen? You okay?"

The combination of preoccupation and the dislodging of the contraption had left him looking like an absent minded professor with bedhead. It was captivating and cute.

His eyes jerked up to meet Rosie's. "I'm gone for you."

Her lips parted. "Glen."

He put the head light down and pulled her down so that she sat next to him, thighs touching. She could feel his breath on her cheek. "There's something I have to tell you."

"Okay." She sounded just as breathless as she felt. She didn't want to feel anxious about what was happening, but Glen wasn't acting like himself.

"I declared for knighthood. I'm in."

She stared into his eyes trying to process. She hadn't known what he was going to say, but she wasn't prepared for that.

"What?"

"One of the members of Z Team retired. I'm taking his place."

"You're not." She said it so quietly it almost sounded like it was coming from somebody else.

"I am. I've been training for this for a long time and I need…"

She stood up quickly. "No." She shook her head. "That's not… You can't."

"Look, baby. I'm not saying I'm doing it

forever. I'm just saying I'm not ready for a desk job. You know?"

"No. I don't know. Why are you telling me this? Is it like a this-sure-was-fun-have-a-nice-life talk?"

"No! I… I don't know exactly. I guess it's a can-we-talk-about-this talk." He felt his stomach muscles clench when he saw a big tear roll down her cheek and, for a moment, he was considering second thoughts.

"Well, you must have had something in mind, Glen. Break it down. Let's say that you're going to Marrakesh. Z Team is getting you instead of the sixty public lashes they deserve."

"Whoa."

"What, exactly, do you see me doing while you're there?" Glen stared at Rosie for a couple of beats and then dropped his gaze. "Son. Of. A. Bitch. You chose that over me."

She continued to stare at Glen, but he wouldn't look at her.

"It's Tuesday, three a.m. at home in California. If you change your mind before supper Thursday, maybe decide it's me instead, let me know. Otherwise, fair warning, I'll be gone. You won't get another chance."

She stood up, but he still didn't look at her.

"Coward," was all she said before she vanished.

Glen sat on the edge of the bed for the next hour without finding the motivation to move other than to breathe in and out. Finally he reached for his phone and dialed Simon.

"I need a ride."

Victoria Danann

CHAPTER 4

"E'en, your Highness. Mr. Innes is here and havin' whiskey at your table."

The manager of the Highlander Club took Duff's coat.

The prince smiled in greeting. "Thank you, Aels. I know the way."

"Very good, sir."

Duff descended the stairs to the wine room. His guest looked up when he heard the seal of the door swish open.

"Duffy!"

"Pey. You can no' possibly have grown as respectable as you look."

His friend scowled. "Of course no'. What do you take me for?"

After a one-armed embrace during which Peyton Innes never relinquished hold of his whiskey glass, they sat in companionable warmth. Peyton was the older brother, by three years, of one of Duff's closest friends. He was big and ruddy and redheaded and gave every impression of being fearless. He'd gone into law and had been with an old legacy Edinburgh firm since graduation.

"Shall I ask how've you been or shall I ask what sort of solicitor services you're in urgent need of?"

Duff smiled. "For now, let me just ask, how you've been?"

"Fine, Duff. Yourself?"

"Well. Your mate?"

"All will be well if I'm home before the clock strikes eight and no' smellin' like I've been makin' love to Scotch."

Duff laughed and glanced at the tumbler. "Should I be takin' that from you then?"

"Only if I begin demandin' another."

After a few seconds of quiet, Duff said, "About the question of respectability…"

"Aye?"

"I'm hirin' you to perform a few services on my behalf. I must know that you will be holdin' the legal tradition of confidentiality sacred. I'll be needin' your word that I can count on that."

Innes set his glass down and sat back in his chair as he gave Duff a professional look of appraisal. "Well, Duffy, I must be askin' you a couple of things first. You know the law as well as I do. There are legal exceptions to confidentiality, as you are aware, and I'm previously bound by a partnership trust that supersedes any vow I would now make to you.

"Under the circumstances I would normally ask two thin's, but in your case the first would no' seem to apply. You are no' likely to be involved in the pursuit of tax evasion since taxes are paid to you indirectly through your family. As to the second thin', will any money launderin' activity be involved?"

Before Duff could respond, the door opened was held open by the club manager while two servers delivered the mutton and potatoes, cooked and dressed to perfection, and served it on hand-painted pottery plates picturing a red stag leaping through a ring of heather. Duff didn't need to glance at his watch to know that Aels would have made sure the request for service at six-fifteen was honored.

When the staff was gone, the room seemed very quiet of a sudden. Not wanting the moment to become awkward, Innes picked up knife and fork and cut into his meat. "Nothin' like a ripe mutton, eh, Duff? Looks lovely indeed."

"Aye. Most appealin'. As to the question put before me just ahead of the lamb's arrival," the prince held up his right hand in a mock taking of oath, "the answer is no, Pey. No money launderin' activity is associated with anythin' I may be askin' about."

Innes stopped and looked Duff full in the face with the sort of sincerity that Scots are known for. "In that case, my answer is aye. Certainly you have my word, little brother. 'Twould be yours whether I was bound by the legal profession or not."

"Thank you, Pey. When all 'tis done, I hope you'll still be callin' me brother."

When Duff reached the top of the third floor stairwell and turned he could see the light in the outer offices at the end of the hall. He didn't go out of his way to sneak up on his assistant, but the man was focused on his task to the exclusion of all else.

"Grieve."

As expected, Grieve cleared at least three inches from the seat of his chair when Duff said his name and clutched at his lapel near his heart. "Sir," he panted.

"Grieve, are you goin' deaf, man? I was no' exactly bein' stealthy on my approach."

"Perhaps, your Highness. I shall look into it."

"What are you doin' here so late?"

Grieve looked at his watch. "'Tis only eight."

"Aye. What time did you arrive this mornin'?"

"Seven thirty, sir."

"I see." Duff sighed. "I do no' deserve you, Grieve. But do you no' have a hobby or any, em, thin's of interest outside this room?"

Grieve looked mystified. "What could be of more interest than affairs of state, sir?"

"Indeed, Grieve. Carry on."

"Aye, sir."

"Oh."

"Sir?"

"About my schedule? Heavy as you please tomorrow, but clear the pages from then till Monday mornin'."

"Sir?" Grieve's eyes were big as he blinked like an owl.

"I'm takin' some personal time, Grieve."

"Personal time, sir?"

"Aye. 'Tis what Americans call it. You may use me as you wish tomorrow. Dawn to midnight. I will skip meals if necessary."

"Oh, sir, I do no' think 'twould be…"

"But! Tomorrow night at midnight, I do no' serve at the pleasure of the fae again until Monday."

"I see, sir. A most unusual idea."

"Aye. And that bein' the case, 'twill be no need to mention it to anyone."

"I understand, sir."

"Good night, Grieve." Duff nodded and continued on toward his personal rooms feeling a little guilty about the worried look on Grieve's face.

As many of the Thursday and Friday appointments as possible were moved to Wednesday and every second of Duff's day was booked to the point where the hallway leading to his office was lined with people waiting like Washington D.C. Congressional lobby cues. Now and then it occurred to Duff that Grieve might have been enjoying himself, having taken instructions quite literally.

When the hall was empty it was just after nine o'clock. Grieve poked his head in.

"That was the last of them, sir. Your calendar is clear till Monday mornin' for, em, personal time."

Duff looked up. "Good job, Grieve. I do no' want to see you till then."

Grieve looked shocked. "But sir! I have work!"

"Then take it home. You are no' to set foot in this place before Monday mornin'. If you attempt to do so, I will have security give you the bum's rush."

"Sir!" Clearly the image of being taken by the seat of the pants was enough to make him feel outraged, which was exactly the reaction Duff was hoping for.

Duff tapped his watch. "Monday mornin'."

Duff ran down to the kitchens to see what there might be to eat. Grieve may have initially protested the idea of booking appointments right through mealtimes, but had scheduled him with no break for the entire day. The kitchen staff had already cleaned up from dinner, but the coolers were stocked full and it wasn't much trouble to put together a respectable plate of cold cuts, cheeses, fruits and bread. He sat at a twenty-foot-long stainless steel preparation table and ate alone, amazed at how good food tastes when the first meal of the day is eaten very late in the day.

While he ate with his hands he began planning the next day, feeling a little giddy about being on his own. That alone was cause for celebration. He went back for a second helping of shortbread and washed it down with pale ale. He looked around the immense, dimly lit kitchen. He had a full tummy and was feeling a little bit tired from a day of too many people wanting too many things, and a little bit cranky about the fact that Grieve had clearly wanted to make sure that it didn't happen often. But underneath all that was something else. Some sensation that wasn't there before. It was sort of pleasant and sort of warm. One minute it was butterflies in the stomach. The next minute it might be an inexplicably stimulated groin. Anticipation maybe.

He gathered up a store of snacks - cheese, shortbread, beer, nuts, and a variety of sweets he probably shouldn't consume, and headed upstairs to his version of a lockdown retreat.

Sitting at his desk in his bedroom with a portaputer, a bagel and lox and maps spread all across his floor and his bed, Duff was enjoying a rare and profound sense of freedom. He had closed and locked the outer office doors, the inner office doors, the sitting room doors and withdrawn into his own private chambers with no one expecting to see him again until Monday. Even so, he sat barefoot on the side of an immaculately made bed – a holdover from his days of rigid military school training no doubt - wearing jeans and a navy blue long sleeve tee with a Strathclyde emblem.

Pulling out his phone, he scrolled down his list of contacts. He knew there was no one else in the room, but looked around anyway. It was enormous. Of course. A rectangular shape perhaps forty feet by thirty feet with a fireplace as tall as he and ten feet wide. At the end of the room a bank of east facing casement windows showcased rain being splashed by wind currents. The entire room and everything in it was a very pale sage green.

Monochrome. Just like my life. But 'tis about to change. Forever.

He selected IAY, send message, then texted, *Sunday 10pm.* It was their method of making a phone date. He looked at the curious response and took a deep breath. *ok xoxo*

Step One. *Asylum*

He set the phone down and got to work on the task list. It was taking shape in his mind. He'd spent a sleepless night running through various scenarios, playing them out in a series of events that always ended the same. In disaster. He didn't have a clear winner, meaning a plan with no risk. What he did have was a plan with the big risk preloaded up front. If he could get past the big gamble he was about to make, the rest was just a matter of list making.

His chief worry was making decisions for Aelsong without her agreement because half their fate was hers, but right or wrong, sometime near dawn he'd decided that's exactly what he would do.

With hours to kill until it was nine a.m. in Ottawa, he began making lists to keep himself busy in the meantime. Around noon he got hungry. The last thing he wanted was to run into somebody who wanted something, which meant the kitchen was out of the question. Too many people likely to ask the wrong things. What was he doing? Why was he dressed like that? Why wasn't he at work? Where was Grieve? Didn't he have a lunch appointment?

So he pulled the hoodie up over his head and ran down the back stairs two flights to the tour guides' break room, which was an obscure little nook tucked into a corner and typically unnoticed by anyone but those who used it. Of course he knew every cranny. Any child left to his own devices for any length of time knows everything about his home including the contents of every drawer and cupboard.

The tour guides, mostly university students who worked part time showing off the bits of the palace that were open to the public, couldn't have been more shocked when the prince burst in, shut the door behind him and leaned against it like someone was after him. As soon as they recovered they all stood.

He looked at the curious faces and half-eaten

sandwiches. "I'm sorry to be disturbin' what appears to be a very fine lunch. Please do no' mind me. Just pretend that I'm no' here." At that, they looked at each other, some more wide-eyed than others. He pointed at the door. "I'm, em, waitin' for a pizza delivery."

With theatrical timing as perfect as a director's cue, there was a knock on the door. Duff nodded in that direction in a gesture meaning, "Go ahead. Open it. "

It was not a door that was used as an entrance or exit. Ever. But a young elf wearing a kilt in MacKesson tartan, pulled it open to find a pizza deliveryman. It was a testament to Duff's directions that he'd found it at all and an even greater feat that he'd managed to get past the palace detail. But there he stood in a Mac under a shallow portico with sheets of rain forming watery walls on three sides.

Duff came forward, took the pizza and thanked the deliveryman who stood with mouth open. "You're the prince, ain't ye?"

"No. I just play him on TV."

"Oh. Well. That'll be eight pound thirty."

Duff almost looked surprised, reached into his pockets and realized he hadn't brought money down. He hadn't thought about it since he didn't normally carry money around his own house.

He looked up at the poor man who had braved a deluge in hopes of a nice tip by a palace occupant and looked around at the young expectant faces as mortification set in. "I'm, ah, sorry. I'm afraid I…"

The lad who had taken it upon himself to act as doorman came to his aid. "'Tis quite alright, your

Highness. Please allow me to buy you lunch."

"Oh, that's very decent of you, kind even, but I could no' impose…"

"No' in the least. I shall ne'er be without a story to tell again," he chuckled.

"No," said a red-haired girl who had found her voice and was advancing from the corner. "The prince's pizza pie will be on me! I insist."

As the argument ensued the prince backed away. When he reached the door, he said, "Thank you for your kindness. Allow me to invite you all to dinner in the Stirlin' room. Monday night at eight." He counted in the air. "Seven. How many would like to plus one?" Every one raised a hand. He smiled. "Very well. Fourteen it is. I'll be leavin' word at the front door."

Duff raced upstairs. The smell was driving him crazy. Truthfully he'd never had a bite of pizza before in his entire life, but it was a day for new possibilities and celebrating the beauty of common things. He relocked every door on his way back to his room, opened a beer, and bit into a pepperoni, Italian sausage, mushroom, black olive and green pepper pizza. He hadn't known what to order so he'd asked the girl who took the order for a suggestion. He groaned out loud. He had eaten in most Relaix Fontaineau restaurants in the world and couldn't remember groaning out loud.

He was glad he'd ordered a large pizza and was already planning on getting another for dinner. He stuffed some currency into his pocket while he was thinking about it.

Sometime later he realized he wasn't hearing rain anymore. He glanced at the windows and then at the clock. He'd gotten so lost in the mechanics of planning a future that he'd gone past his target time. No matter. Later was probably better.

The where had come to him with the simple random action of the turn of a globe on the way past. Canada was the world's second largest country. If he and Song wore caps or wore their hair over their ears, with their coloring, in most places they could blend in.

Canadians spoke a version of the same language. It was cold. True. But they were both from the same latitude as the southern half of Canada so weather wasn't the issue that it might be for some. Lots of beautiful, sparsely populated land. It might not be heaven, but close enough. Be it ruinous or fortuitous, he would let their future ride on the casual spin of the globe.

Duff had met the Canadian Prime Minister at a state dinner a few months before and, in all modesty, she had seemed taken with him. She'd made a point of remarking that, seeing him in person, she certainly understood why he'd been named World's Sexiest Bachelor.

He knew her response to his request for sanctuary would depend on a variety of factors. The granting of political sanctuary would draw worldwide attention and Canada was not known for being at the center of mediating international affairs. It could cement the office on her behalf until she died or decided to resign. Or it could shorten her political career and become the entire character of her legacy. Much would depend on her mood and personal ambition, both of which could only be known by the Prime Minister herself.

He hoped his voice wouldn't shake. It wouldn't normally have occurred to him except that, when he lifted the phone, he noticed his hand was shaking a little. He had a lot riding on that one phone call.

After talking with three levels of bureaucrats, Duff was put through. "Madame Prime Minister."

"Your Highness. To what do I owe the honor?"

"My mate and I want to be citizens of your beautiful country. We are formally requestin' political asylum. We will no' be a drain on public resources. We have the means to support ourselves."

Fifteen minutes later, Duff had spelled out the issues and the need for asylum.

"If you can get here unaided, you'll be granted asylum."

She promised that their conversation would not be leaked until after Song and Duff were safe on Canadian soil. He said that he would confirm with her the exact date and place when they would arrive.

Step Two. *Pick a GO DATE.*
Materials needed: calendar.

There will never be a perfect time. Looking for a perfect time equals procrastination. Procrastination is the first step toward failure. Best chance of success. Pick a self-imposed, hard deadline.

He looked at the calendar. It was March third. His eyes drifted downward. March fifteenth caught his eye. His mouth twitched. No surprise why. March fifteen marked the end of boar season in Germany. It was one of his favorite things in the world. An area of the Black Forest was maintained as a nature preserve. Every spring they allowed a few dignitaries, on application, to hunt *without* modern weapons, during the very short season, to keep the population manageable.

Duff hadn't been in two years. He looked up and laughed out loud. *Perfect.*

He grabbed his phone, ran through his contacts and tapped the screen. It rang.

"Here."

"'Tis the crown callin' for back taxes."

"Duffy! You sod! Your old man's bleedin' me dry, I tell ye. So you can no' be too poor to hire cute lassies to dun poor citizens out of their rightful earnin's?"

"Cute lassies, you say? Have you seen Grieve?"

"'Tis damn hard to be you."

"Aye. I've always said as much. Strange that 'twould take a tax collection call to make you see." The reply was good-natured laughter. "So would you happen to know what month 'tis?"

"'Tis pig stickin' month."

"Aye. 'Tis. Hard to get one past you, Iwan. Can you get away?"

"Believe I might. What are you thinkin'?"

"I'm thinkin' do a favor, get a favor."

"Oh? Let's hear it then."

"Well, I need to be somewhere that is no' here without explainin' to anyone, particularly my mother, where that might be, if you're understandin' what I mean."

"I believe I do."

"So I thought I might say I've gone huntin' with the boys."

"Aye. Duffy, I will cover your ass should it become necessary and you know you do no' even have to ask it, e'en though lyin' to the queen is probably a hangin' offense. But..."

"But?"

"I imagine it goes without sayin'. You're no fifteen, you know."

He sighed deeply. "Ah, Iwan. All jokin' aside. Bein' prince is complicated."

"Well, we already established 'tis hard to be you. Tell me the details."

After they discussed who might go and when they would leave, Duff hung up making a mental note to do something special for Iwan no matter how things turned out. Step Two complete.

Go date: *March 10th*
To Do:
1.) Arrange clearance for hunting party with German ambassador.

2.) Have Grieve clear my calendar from March 10th through 16th.

3.) Have Song tell The Order she will be going home for personal time.

Step Three. *Getting away.*
Goal: *To be there before they know we're gone.*
Needed: 1.) passports and travel documents 2.) transportation

To Do:
    1.) Arrange transportation.
    2.) Inform PM when itinerary is set.

Step Four. *A new life.*
Needed: 1.) money 2.) place to live

Duff thanked the gods that he was one of the one percent of the one percent who need not worry about money. His grandfather, on passing, had left him a trust that had matured on Duff's twenty-fifth birthday. He'd never touched a penny of it. Never so much as thought about it. But there was enough there to support a couple for a lifetime if they lived a reasonably humble lifestyle.

At times in his life he'd wondered if he should feel guilty because he knew that extreme privilege or power almost always began with plunder, but he'd had more opportunity to curse his ancestors for their success with war and coastal raiding than thank them for it.

Wanting to reach Innes before office hours ended Friday, Duff called with his list.

"You ready?"

"Go."

"I need to move my trust to Canada."

"Have you given thought as to how you'll be wantin' to do that?"

"I have. I was thinkin' to have you rush through purchase of a legacy corp, then open a bank account with Scotiabank in Canada with myself as signatory and transfer the balance from RBS."

"Hmmm. That would work. It will also cost a fortune."

"'Tis fortunate I have one then. And it needs to be accomplished by next Wednesday."

"Well, Duffy, you never were one for lettin' grass grow under your feet."

"Take it as a compliment that I chose you then, Pey."

"'Tis. Indeed. Still, could be tricky. Next."

"I'll be wantin' you to make some purchases on my behalf. First, I want a very specific plane. A Tecnam P2006T. Call the plant in Capua. They have a wait list, but perhaps sufficient incentive could insure delivery to an out of the way private hanger in Aberdeen by Thursday early mornin'. With prepurchase inspections completed, maintenance check, fueled up and ready to go. Of course."

"Of course." Innes sighed heavily. "Thursday, you say. I feel a weekend in the office comin' on."

"Were you sayin' you're ready for the next item?"

"Aye. You heard right."

"I would like to acquire some property in Canada. I believe it would be most expedient if the corporation purchases it on my behalf?"

"As a recap, I understand you want the corporation in place *with* money transferred by Wednesday. In the most unlikely event I am able to perform miracles and brin' this to pass, when are you hopin' to transfer the property into the portfolio of your Canadian corporation?"

"Well, if you have a willin' seller and a willin' buyer and an unencumbered title and a local lawyer who can use a printer, then I see no reason why it could no' be accomplished on Thursday."

"I'm a solicitor, Duff. No' a sorcerer."

"Really?"

"Aye."

"Do you recall the strawberry blonde you pulled out of the hat check in London?"

"Duff!" he said with a tone of warning. "There are certain thin's friends are supposed to forget once their friends are well and truly mated."

"Where is that written?"

"It does no' need to be written to be true and I predict that I shall be remindin' you of this conversation soon enough with a few recollections of my own."

"Thor's Brows, simmer down, I'm givin' your folly a twirl. 'Tis a bit more wiggle room on the closin' of the real property. Say, Tuesday. Wednesday latest."

"Well, at least it seems more within the realm of reality, which is where my legal practice is most comfortable. And, on the subject, since you have hired me as your personal solicitor, the capacity of advisor bein' implied, I behooves me to be askin' certain questions."

"Such as."

"Do you want to tell me what this is all about?"

"I do, Pey, very much. But that information will no' be forthcomin'."

After a pause, Innes said, "All right. Do you have the information on the real property?"

"No' yet. I'm doin' research online and will have a list of possibilities for you to look into, say, noon tomorrow. I do no' want to communicate by email. I'll type out the URLs and maybe you could come pick them up."

"Come pick up URLs?"

"Aye." Duff gave him directions. "Oh. And bring a pizza."

"A pizza?" Innes sounded like he wasn't sure what it was.

"Aye. I like the round sort of pepper sausage thin's. Whatever you want will be fine."

"All right, Duff." Innes bore the indulgent tone of a man set on a visit with a friend committed to an institution.

Duff closed the phone. He'd been staring at the monitor with the Tecnam P2006T specs on it while he was talking to Innes. Once he knew where he and Song were going, it hadn't taken long to reason out that their best chance was to be gone before anyone knew it. With a face as readily recognizable as his, that made leaving the country a problem by air, sea, or rail. Unless he could get away by private plane.

If he showed up at a large airport terminal, paparazzi would be everywhere. If he chartered a private jet, it would hit the entertainment news and speculation about use of the phrase "playboy" was bound to arise and draw attention. However, if he showed up at a small hangar to try out the new twin engine plane of a friend, he could drive right onto the tarmac and might even sneak into the cockpit without being noticed.

Duff had gotten his pilot's license when he was fourteen. He loved flying and, in another life, might have found a way to make a living at doing that instead of being a professional manikin, available for photo shoots with sports teams, or the token royal entertaining officials at lunches.

The plane he was staring at was perfect in every way. It was a gorgeous twin engine, high wing, retractable gear beauty with Garmin glass instrumentation. Stable. Responsive. Sleek. Lightweight. Fast. It only needed a thousand feet of runway or, in a pinch, a stretch of smooth fairway.

The view of the interior with its modern molding and classic instruments was romantic. He could so easily picture eloping in that plane. He envisioned the beautiful elf with the bright blue eyes and the luscious smile sitting just inches away, looking breathless about an unknown future, but so happy that they were facing it together just inches apart.

He pulled his attention back to the task at hand. When lovers are fleeing, they need an exact destination. Canada is far too general. Second, they need a flight plan. He decided to work on finding a place to live property first.

It took longer than he thought - all night, in

fact, but when it was done, he had something to give Peyton. Three choices, but the second and third were far below number one. He had his heart set on the first and hoped it didn't turn out to be an old, cached, expired listing. With luck it would turn out to be already vacated or arrangements could be made to prepare for new owners immediately.

He'd started out looking just on the other side of the Atlantic Ocean, but some urge kept driving him further west until he'd gone almost to the other side of the world. That's when he found it, the very thing that made his heart sing. There was a picture of the Canadian Rockies and the river that meandered in front of what he hoped would be his future home.

A hundred and seventy-four acres of timberland on the Fraser River near McBride, BC, bordering on park land, about one hundred fifty miles from Prince George to the west and one hundred fifty miles from Jasper to the east. One thing was for sure. No one would be doing a casual drive by to say hello.

The description said the year round off-grid home was solar/wind powered with a diesel generator as backup. The main wood stove was located downstairs, with the kitchen cook stove upstairs, which also heated water, so there would be a continuous supply of hot and cold running water.

It also went into great detail about the attached greenhouse that allowed early gardening. "Eat salads before the snow is off the ground," it said. As for outdoor gardening, it described separate gardens of established strawberries, asparagus, and assorted other berries as well as an herb garden, large vegetable garden complete with removable hoop houses for earlier planting, and an apple orchard.

Among the wildlife mentioned were moose, elk, deer, bear, wolves, coyotes, and migratory birds.

He hadn't known it was possible to want something so badly it made your teeth hurt. Other than Song, of course. He'd never had a chance to ask how she might feel about any of it, but he knew how she felt about living apart. He wondered what she would think about growing strawberries. He wondered if she even liked strawberries. He looked at his watch. It was the wee hours. He wished he could just pick up the phone, call and ask if she liked strawberries. As for himself, he liked them fine, but wasn't sure if they grew on a tree or bush or vine.

He got a few hours' sleep, and woke just in time to go greet Innes. He didn't have time to shave and knew he looked unkempt. He hadn't had proper dinner, hadn't had any breakfast, but he felt great.

He pulled up his hoodie, ran down the two flights of back stairs and burst in on the tour guides right at noon. They stopped eating, stopped talking, rose from their seats quickly and stared, but didn't look nearly as surprised as they had the day before.

He could see that they were waiting for some bit of courteous pleasantry. He mulled over what that might be and, at length, settled on, "Good afternoon."

Collectively they nodded and murmured, "Good afternoon," like an en masse responsive reading.

"Please do no' let me interrupt again. I'm just meetin' a friend." He smiled. "For a pizza." He shrugged. "But no worries. I brought money." He waved some bills.

They neither moved nor said anything in return, but did look at each other. Again, there was a knock on the door as if on cue. The same young elf rose to open it. It was raining even harder than the day before.

Innes was standing there in an elegant black waxed coat with water pouring off him as the shallow portico couldn't protect him from windblown rain. He was holding a cardboard pizza box with a bit of plastic over it as haphazard protection and looked as pitiful as a stray dog.

"Come in, man," Duff said as he motioned him forward. Innes stepped inside and nodded to the little assembly. "These are some of our finest tour guides. 'Tis little doubt that each of them knows infinitely more about my family tree than do I. I'm afraid I've interrupted their noon meal two days in a row now."

They all rushed to say, "No. No' at all, your Highness. 'Twas a pleasure."

"This is my friend and solicitor, Mr. Innes. If you'll excuse us, we'll just…" Looking at Innes, Duff stopped. "Perhaps you'd like to leave your wrapper here? The gang will look after it for ye."

He looked up at the guides for confirmation. They all rushed to assure Mr. Innes that his coat would be safe with them. So Duff took the pizza and ran off leaving his solicitor to struggle out of his coat and give chase like they were boys.

By the time they reached Duff's suites, Innes was so red faced and heaving Duff was concerned he may have done the man injury.

"Peyton. Fae's gods, man. I could no' have

dreamed you'd let yourself go or I never would have tested ye. Please accept my apology. And, when you can once again draw breath, I'll offer you a beer to go with your pizza."

"Very funny. If I had lost sight of you in this damned infernal place, I may have been wanderin' about for days before bein' found, only then to be imprisoned because of no' bein' able to properly explain what I was doin' here. Deliverin' a pizza to the prince! A likely story indeed, solicitor.

"My mate would be told I was found lookin' like a drowned rat goin' door to door sayin', 'Duffy? Duffy?' You should be ashamed of yourself." Duff just laughed. "You know, Duff Torquil, what you're needin' is a mate. Settle you right down by all the gods."

"Right you are, Pey, and I'll be agreein' to the marrow in my very bones."

"You will?"

"Aye."

"Are you goin' to eat that whole thin' by yourself or were you plannin' to share?"

During pizza and beer, Innes took a look around at the state of Duff's bedroom with maps and papers strewn everywhere, also noting the dark circles under his eyes and the two days growth of beard.

"Duffy. Can't help noticin' there's a lot of movin' parts bein' put into play here. Also can no' help noticin' that your groomin' is in a wee state of decline."

"Just a minor speed bump while I work out

details. No' to worry. In fact, in many ways I have ne'er been better. Do your part in this and I'll be eternally grateful in ways that mere fees can no' express."

"A sweet speech, lad. But I am worried nonetheless."

Shaking his head, the prince motioned toward the door. "Come let me show you the way out. I can no' have you gettin' lost," he laughed. When they reached the guides' break room, they shook hands outside the door.

Duff said, "Call or text me as soon as you have some good news."

He was referring to the British Columbia property that Duff had shown him online. As the prince had rightly said, people in the business of buying and selling real estate were actively engaged in commerce on weekends.

Back in his room, alone again, Duff was thinking Innes was right. There were a lot of moving parts, which meant there were a lot of things that could go wrong, which meant that he had to be excruciatingly meticulous about every detail. He went back to work planning the last big step. How to get there.

He spread the biggest maps he could find out across the floor and then set the portaputer down on top of that with his notebook, ready to start the flight plan. He smiled to himself.

Before the days of airplanes, the word flight was only used in reference to humans to describe fleeing. As Duff planned their escape it occurred to him that both meanings of flight applied to their elopement.

They were fleeing by flying.

How he wished she was with him.

Right then.

He wished she was sitting next to him on his bedroom floor helping to calculate the flight plan as they conspired together about their getaway, imagining their new life, whispering about strawberries and caribou between kisses and touches while the rain beat against the casement windows of the northeast wing where fae royalty had slept and made more royal fae for three hundred years.

The critical calculations began with cruising speed, which fully loaded and fueled would average a hundred fifty-five miles per hour. Cumulative endurance range equaled four hours or seven hundred thirteen miles. In layman terms, that meant whatever came first.

He had to calculate what "fully loaded" meant, which included Aelsong's weight. He knew it would be hopeless to ask her that and trust that the answer would be correct. He did know a little about females. So the only way to solve that problem was with a guess.

Day One.

Starting with Aberdeen, ninety-two miles from where he sat, they would take off from a small airfield and be over land for about fifteen minutes, over the North Sea for about fifteen minutes, over the highlands of Scotia for another fifteen minutes and then they would be flying north by northwest over the Norwegian Sea en route to the Faroe Islands.

The Faroes were under Danish sovereignty, which could not be better for Duff. He and the Danish prince had both been educated at Eton and had gotten along well. If there was any issue at the airstrip in the Faroes, a phone call would resolve it. Three hundred sixty-eight miles. A little over two hours.

Of course he could go further, but they needed to stop because of the way the next two legs would play out. If they didn't spend the night in the Faroes, they'd be forced to stop at Rekjavik where he would be recognized and pandemonium would follow. They had to get to Canada before the hounds of Hades, otherwise known as paparazzi, were set free. And, he thought, they could do worse than a staggeringly beautiful, like-nowhere-else-on-Earth stop for their first night together.

That stopped his train of thought in its tracks. His first night with his mate, the first time he would make love to her for that matter, would be the Faroe Islands in the middle of the Norwegian Sea. Keeping that in mind he started scanning available lodging.

Since it was a far cry from tourist season, there was plenty available. He found a guesthouse described as unpretentious, honest and delightful. "Read between the lines," he muttered to himself, at the same time thinking plain was okay. He and his intended were beyond being impressed by luxury. He jotted down the info including a note on the private annex building which he would send off to Innes so that arrangements could be made that were not traceable back to him.

Day Two.

They would make a stop for fuel, a piddle and food in Iceland, which was the only real worry. Keeping their heads down, weather and gods willing, they would get as far as the Kalusuk settlement at Tasiilaq, Eastern Greenland on the Denmark Strait just south of the Arctic Circle before dark and spend the night in a cold, but truly picturesque village.

Greenland was politically neutral and not a concern.

Day Three.

Stop for fuel, food and a piddle at Igaluit, Canadian Territory, Arctic. On to Happy Valley-Goose Bay, Newfoundland and Labrador. Stop for the night.

From the time they reached Igaluit they would be able to breathe easy because, even if no formal announcement had been made, they would be under protection of the Canadian government and could not be reclaimed by the Irish and Scotia monarchies without Canada's permission.

Day Four.

Make it to Quebec by two o'clock where the Prime Minister would meet them. The Prime Minister would have an escort waiting at the airport and a press conference set up at the Fairmont Le Chateau Frontenac. From that time on, the world would know.

It was anybody's guess whether the families would demand they return or simply disown them.

Day Five.

They would continue their journey to Winnepeg with a stop in Sault Ste Marie. He would ask the Prime Minister for a small security detail just to be sure that they could get to a hotel and back to the airport without a problem.

Day Six.

Stop in Saskatoon then on to Prince George where a hangar had been leased for the plane. The hangar came with a little hostel style efficiency in the back where they could spend the night.

Day Seven.

Buy two cars. Buy supplies. Drive a hundred and fifty miles to McBride and start settling into their new home.

There it was. What could go wrong? A lot.
As to how to anticipate every eventuality and put a Plan B in place, that was easy. Give up. It couldn't be done. The Fates claim their share of outcomes in spite of the best of plans. And that's that.

CHAPTER 5

Duff spent most of Sunday pacing up and down, going over it all again and again looking for flaws. He was also giving himself a crash course on things most people take for granted like budgeting money, trying to decide how much you can spend after you pay for necessities, which Duff had never thought about. Ever.

It was a whole new world. And it was exciting.

There were so many unknowns. He didn't know if they'd be well-received, if the locals would get used to them, accept them and allow them to simply live their lives. He stopped in front of the mantel whereupon sat a collection of photos. He couldn't say he'd miss his father at all, but he did feel pangs of both guilt and sadness about leaving without telling his mother goodbye.

He was so antsy by nine thirty that he couldn't stay indoors anymore. If he was caught leaving the palace, there would be the devil to pay. If he wasn't mobbed, then he certainly would get the speech about the dangers of going about with security, meaning assassination or kidnapping. He put on a black skull cap that covered his hair, pulled a navy hoodie low over his brow, and kept his head down.

It was dark. It was late. It was Sunday night in early March. There were not that many people out and about and those that were would not be expecting the prince of the fae to be out walking alone late at night. So he stuck his hands in the fleecy front pouch and took a brisk jog up Calton Hill. There was nobody up there but an old man walking a dog.

It wasn't quite ten, but he couldn't wait a minute longer. He took a chance that she was as eager as he and already situated somewhere private to accept his call.

"My love."

He closed his eyes when he heard her voice, like a lick of honey.

"There you are."

"Here I am."

"Do you know how hard it was to find out what xoxo means?"

She laughed and the sound pulled all his nerve endings up tight like she was the symphony conductor and his body was a collection of instruments for her to play.

"'Twas a puzzle then?"

"Aye. And I was already too busy gettin' us away from here." There was no response except that he thought he might have heard a little catch in her breathing. Finally, he said, "Song? Do you hear me?"

She started to say his name, but her voice did break and then she was crying. "Duffy. Are we really goin' then?"

He didn't know exactly what he'd been expecting, but he hadn't expected tears. He sat down on a bench that was cold through his jeans. "Thursday mornin' early. You tell The Order you're goin' home for a visit. Pack your warmest. 'Tis really cold where we're goin'. And take your keepsakes cause we can no' know for sure we'll be comin' back."

"I know."

"Be sure. 'Tis a bell we can no' unring. You can say no, but do it now."

"Stop your teasin', Duff. 'Tis you I'm wantin' and no other. And ye know it."

His chest filled with the burn of that. "If what you're describin' is only a little of what I'm feelin'... Be ready to go by seven. I'm havin' someone drive you to Aberdeen. I'll be waitin' for you there."

"Someone? Who?"

He smiled. "Someone with outrageous pink hair who's married to your brother." Pause. "Speechless, are ye? I have a feelin' I should relish these times as they may be few and far between."

"'Tis easy to say when you're standin' who knows where? 'Twill be a sight different when I can get my hands on you."

Duff lowered his voice. "Aye. 'Twill be different when *I* can get my hands on *you*."

The words hung in the air with all the promise, anticipation, and excitement of fanfare. Her body recognized his meaning and tone and responded with a shiver that was more like a quake. If she had known that he was standing atop Calton Hill, and that a dash out the door, down the street, five blocks and a breathless run straight up could bring her into his arms, she wouldn't have been able to stop herself. She took a deep breath and let it out. "Aye. Agree."

"Song."

"Aye, love."

"Do no' forget your passport."

"I will no'."

"Four days. Will ne'er be without you again."

"Four days."

Song didn't need as much as two seconds to regret leaving her job at The Order just as she hadn't hesitated to accept when she'd initially been approached by the recruiter. Her brother had never talked to her about his life, what he did, the organization or anything about it, of course, but her talent enabled her to see quite a lot. She'd been dazzled by the idea of being a cog in a wheel of such monumental importance and, though she might not ever be a legendary vampire slayer like her brother, she was eager to make a difference with her own gift.

She had spent the entire time in testing. Not doing testing, being tested. A year and a half later, she had not been called upon to do one thing of consequence other than the Alternate-Storm project for which she was specifically requested, by name, by the temporary acting head of Jefferson Unit, Glendennon Catch. As soon as the results were compiled and filed, she was sent right back to testing and all resumed, as if the trip to New Jersey had been a dream. Nothing had changed. At all.

Elora had to do some quick thinking to come up with a plan that would enable her to help her sister-in-law without lying to Rammel outright. She wouldn't be needed at all if it wasn't for the fact that

Aelsong was an elf living in the Fae Kingdom. Otherwise, she could simply walk out the front door, smile at the doorman, and sashay away.

She could do that regardless and, if she never spoke, she'd be safe because certainly no one could tell the difference between elf or fae on sight. But anyone could be alarmed or put in danger and vocalize spontaneously. If she was caught alone and discovered, she would be assumed to be a spy. Someone had to help her get away and Elora was the only candidate.

Fortunately, she was able to talk Litha into combining a short shopping trip to London with a one night stopover at the apartment The Order kept for Storm and Litha at Headquarters in Edinburgh. All Elora had to do was make sure she was there Wednesday night.

With a lot of fast talking about how much she needed a break from Helm and trainees and assassins, it was hard to argue with all that. So Rammel gave his blessings and, of course, Litha provided transportation. After Litha gave the bell service a tip, not much of one because they didn't have any luggage, he closed the door to their suite at the Hyde Park Hotel and left. She walked through the parlor into the bedroom where Elora had sprawled across one of the overdone beds.

"Spill."

"Spill?"

"Right here." Litha pointed to a spot on the rug with her shoe. "Must have tumped the tea cart."

"Oh." Elora got up on an elbow to look.

"No! Not that kind of spill. The kind that

means now is the time to shed the light of truth on what's going on here." Litha waved her arm at their surroundings. "You're not a spend-the-day-at-Harrods kind of girl. You're a shop-online-while-Ram's-watching-rugby-on-TV kind of girl."

"Maybe I did need a couple of days away."

"Maybe you did. But not for shopping." As Litha's eyes narrowed, Elora's got bigger and more innocent looking in inverse proportion. "So what did you need the time away for?"

Elora sniffed and looked away. "I admit it wasn't shopping. Although, now that we're here, we do have to shop since there's no way to ride the passes with luggage."

"Elora."

"Well."

"Spit it out."

"I can't spit it out without implicating you and I need you plausibly ignorant."

Litha took a deep breath that ended with shaking her head and that turned into a chuckle. "I couldn't possibly be more scandalized than to have my best friend think it would be possible for me to be plausibly ignorant. Whatever happened to good old-fashioned plain-Jane ignorance without the modifiers?"

"Okay. So I knew it was unlikely that I'd get this past you. I guess I just hoped you'd let it slide."

"If you need me to play dumb for you, I will. Just as long as you know I'm not dumb and I'm not one of those you're trying to play."

"Oh, for all the gods, Litha." Elora slumped on the bed. "When you say it like that, you make me feel like something that should slither off through the storm drain never to be seen or heard from again. The one I'm trying to protect isn't dumb either."

Litha sat on the other bed facing Elora's. "You kept me propped up when Rosie was on the way. You helped keep things together when Storm was lost. After all that you don't think you could trust me with anything?"

Elora sat up and cocked her head. "Sure. It's not that. Not that at all. It's that I don't want to put you in that position if it isn't necessary. And it's not when you could just be my partner in shopping crime."

Elora's brows were wrinkling in the middle.

Litha smiled. "Okay. Tea and a toes up?"

Elora grinned. "Yeah. It was a hard trip. Are you going to call room service or conjure up the tea?"

"Already checked the closets. No cauldron," Litha deadpanned as she reached for the room service menu.

She set the menu down in her lap.

"What is it?" Elora asked.

"I know where my mother grew up. I even know where I was born and where my people lived for generations. It's funny. I'd never had the slightest desire to go there or even thought of it until just now." She looked closely at Elora. "Would you like to go there with me some time?"

"Of course. I'd love it."

CHAPTER 6

Song pulled her things out into the hallway as quietly as possible to keep from waking her roommate, Gaia. She'd gotten a text from Elora the night before with instructions to meet in the garage beneath the building at seven. The Order kept a small fleet for use of the staff and visitors.

Elora had claimed one of the vehicles, a silver Vauxhall, the most common car in all of Scotia and least likely to draw notice. The sun would just be coming up and Elora wanted to be away from the city before anyone who might recognize Song was likely to see her.

When the elevator opened, Elora was waiting with a big grin on her face. Song started to laugh, but somehow the laughter turned into something that was a confused fusion of crying and laughing. She went as fast as she could rolling the bags she had un-nested and packed for the trip.

Gaia had said, "Seems like you're taking a lot for a trip home. And it's not *that* cold."

Song had lied like she was used to it. "I'm thinkin' of changin' some thin's out. Leave some. Take some. You know."

She dropped the luggage handles and threw her arms around Elora who said, "Quick kiss. We can cry all the way there if you want, but we've got to get started."

They more or less threw her bags in the boot and jumped in. Elora had to produce credentials. She wasn't recognized on sight since she didn't normally drive when she was there. The gate opened. They drove up the incline and out of the garage. When they turned onto the open street, the two women looked at each other and laughed spontaneously like they had just escaped from a prison.

"You know, Song, your brother is the hero. But this may be the most *romantic* moment of the century. How are your map reading skills?"

"Map readin'? Does this automobile no' have geo-guide?"

"No. That's a feature of higher end cars. Um. How's your driving?"

Song grinned. "I'm your girl."

"Maybe we should trade places. You're used to left side anyhow. Makes sense."

"Just past that roundabout, pull over at the market."

That turned out to be easier said than done. After listening to Elora's tirade on roundabouts, Song was all the more sure that she was the one who should be driving.

"Bloody fucking roundabouts! If you go, they honk at you. If you don't go, they honk at you. If you go fast, they honk. If you go slow, they honk. It's just one big bloody honking country full of honking idiot drivers."

Song was laughing when they switched places. "Is that my brother's influence I hear? Ne'er mind. I'm all about the roundabouts. I shall steer the steely beast. You shall navigate."

Aelsong was masterfully at ease with the rules – and quirks – of the road, not to mention gear shift on the left instead of the right. By the time they got to the Forth Road Bridge going north over the water toward Perth, they were speeding along and the tension in their bodies was melting away.

Elora had never taken a road trip in Scotia and was thoroughly enjoying the scenery.

"I suppose you were plannin' to drive back by yourself?"

"I was. Yes. I am. Did you eat before we left? Are you hungry?"

"I did no' eat. I can no' say I'm hungry exactly." She looked over at Elora and smiled shyly. "More nervous, maybe. Should we stop for somethin'?"

"We can't stop and sit down, but maybe we could get take-out."

"We have no' quite perfected the art of to-go like the States. What did you have in mind?"

"I'll settle for a bottle of water and a bag of nuts if I can't do better."

Aelsong looked at her and laughed. Fifteen minutes later they were pulling away from a roadside grill with a to-go breakfast of eggs, lamb goulash for Elora and latte for Song. Elora was ecstatic enough to hum yummy sounds while she ate.

"Do you know where in Aberdeen we're goin'?"

"Hmmm." Elora had finished and was reconciling containers into trash for the backseat floorboard. "It's a row of private plane hangars on the outskirts of the airport. I've got the address and a code to give security when we arrive."

"So we're flyin' somewhere. What else do you know?"

"Not much, Song. I get the feeling that Duff wants to be the one to tell you everything else and, not that it's likely I'll be tortured, but it's probably best I don't know everything." Song nodded. "I've been wondering how you feel about, you know, leaving everything."

" Or everyone?"

"Well, both, I guess."

"I would have left the job regardless." She laughed softly. "To say that it was a dead-end career path would be an understatement. So that is no' a consideration. There are other thin's though… The knowin' I may no' see my family again." She glanced at Elora, then immediately back at the road. "The knowin' I may no' see home again.

"And 'tis almost as hard knowin' the same 'tis true for Duff. I have no idea how hard these thin's will be wearin' on him over time. I can no' say 'tis no' a worry."

"But you don't have a choice, do you?"

Song shook her head and laughed. "But we do no' have a choice, do we?"

They rode in silence for some time, each lost in their own thoughts about what the future might bring, good and bad. A little before nine, Elora's phone rang. She reached down into the bag at her feet and looked at the phone face. It was Glen.

"Hey, Glen. Isn't it either late or early or something for you to be calling?"

"I'm over here, too. Well, Ireland. Not the

same thing, I know. But I've run down that errand for you."

Elora looked over at Song, wondering if the word irony could possibly be accented in a bigger font followed by more exclamation points than she was imagining.

"Thank you. Actually, I'm in a car on a road trip…"

"Oh. If you're driving, I can call back later."

"No. I'm not driving. In fact, what I was going to say is that one of the people concerned with the outcome is in the car with me, driving in fact. I can't reveal the identity of my companion, but I'm going to put the phone on speaker if you don't have any objection."

"None."

"Good. Just a sec."

Song glanced away from the road just long enough to meet Elora's eyes in a questioning way. Elora balanced the phone on the console out of the way of the gear box and said, "Okay, Glen, go ahead."

"I can assume the third party is privy to extra-normal conversations?"

"Yes. You can."

"Right. So you want the long version or the short version?"

Elora looked at her watch. "We've got an hour and full bars."

Glen took a deep breath. "Okay, here goes. Believe it or not the trail led to a hermit in a cave. Weird. Even weirder than it sounds. It was kind of Yoda meets Jack Kerouac."

Elora shook her head like she had the face-to-face feature turned on. "No idea, Glen."

"Never mind. We never would have found the place if it wasn't for Rosie's particular talents. She's like a supernatural hound dog."

"Uh-huh. Did you tell her that?"

"No. And you won't either if you want any more favors." Elora chuckled. "So this guy, the hermit, he's an elf. If you want a picture, he's middle-aged, but good-looking, dressed like a biker of all things. Wasn't especially glad to see us, but he did make tea for Rosie and, when I told him this professor at Oxford named Puddephat sent us, he said he'd talk."

As Glen recounted the story of the migration of the children of Danu to the Briton Isles, Song looked over at Elora from time to time as if to judge her reaction. Elora did the same in return and noticed Song's brow creasing in the middle.

"That's it," he concluded.

"Stunning, Glen. It sounds like this Finrar could be a future candidate for a Nobel Peace Prize."

Glen snorted. "First, show me the peace. Then we'll talk about the prize."

"It's a start and it could be more important than you could begin to guess. To me. To the person I'm with and to," Elora looked at Song and smiled, "all the Dana.

"I owe you one for this. Need just one more thing. Type it up and email it to me? Please?"

"Yeah. Okay. I was going to say you didn't owe me before the typing thing."

Elora chuckled. "See you at home."

"Bye."

Elora closed the phone, put it back in the bag, and looked over at Aelsong whose attention wasn't deviating from the road straight ahead. They were coming into the southern outskirts of Aberdeen and would be swinging west of the city veering toward the airport to the northwest. The traffic had picked up noticeably and the hour was high commerce, both good reasons for Song to be concentrating on driving.

They drove past cultivated fields, industrial parks and golf courses, all managing somehow to coexist in the unlikely presence of the other. Elora took a look at the map to be sure she knew the next turn to expect and then allowed her own thoughts to drift. When Song did speak, it almost startled her.

"So there's no' the hair's difference between us. Elf and fae."

"No. I suspected as much. I had to have a transfusion of a lot of blood to survive and the blood they gave me was fae. I survived. And I haven't had a single impulse to make haggis."

Song did laugh at that. Few could learn to love the haggis once they started taking meals out of a highchair.

"You'd asked Glen to look into the, em, situation?"

"Yes. When I first learned about the hostilities, I asked your brother about the why of it. He didn't have an answer, but I thought that could be simply because history isn't his major area of expertise."

"My brother is thrice blest to have a lovely wife such as yourself, one who puts thin's so delicately," she smirked.

"Well, Song, it's not as if he does not have his areas of expertise. Believe me. He does."

"Takin' your word."

"So more from personal curiosity than anything, I began asking others when the opportunity presented itself. When I couldn't find anyone who knew, I checked online and then even asked the crusties at The Order. Drew a blank."

Song looked confused. "Drew a blank?"

"Hmm? Oh. Sorry. It means I came up with nothing. About the same time, in an enchanting demonstration of synchronicity I noticed the spark that was struck between you and the prince."

"Oh."

"When I talked to Duff at Rammel's Hall of Heroes induction I told him that I would be trying to find an inroad into weakening the obstacles. It's taken a lot longer than I hoped. Your prince got tired of waiting and I don't blame him. Once I knew who Ram was to me, I don't think I could have waited so long." Elora pointed at a sign.

"Take that one north. I think we're only fifteen minutes away."

Song took in a quivering breath. "How do I look?"

Elora looked her over appreciatively. "Beautiful as a bride."

Song's phone rang. "Aye?" Smile. "We're almost there." Pause. "Elora says she thinks fifteen minutes. What am I lookin' for?" Pause. "Hmm. Aye." She hung up then grinned at Elora. "'Tis happenin'."

"Aye. 'Tis," Elora teased her. Aelsong looked worried. "What's wrong?"

"You have a breathmint?"

"Yes." Elora opened a tin and handed it to her. "Um. Ginger."

After one dead end, two illegal u turns, three honks, and a phone call to Duff they saw the Aeromax Hangrow sign and pulled in next to the secured entry. Aelsong just nodded when the guard said, "Good mornin'." He checked IDs against the names on his list and opened the gates. "Follow the yellow line and keep to the right."

As they drove through, Song and Elora both breathed a huge sigh of relief. When they rounded the end of the building, the landscape opened out again. They had a clear view of the tarmac, the landing strip and environs, the hangar row, several small propeller planes that sat invitingly like giant toys, and the figure of a handsome fae prince with his solicitor.

It took some effort to keep from gunning the accelerator, but soon enough the vehicle came to a stop next to a sparkling new plane with steps down. Song put the car in park, but didn't get the ignition turned off before the door was ripped open by an impatient lover. Song was fumbling with the seat belt latch. Elora calmly reached over and released it for her, then turned off the ignition.

He pulled her into his arms and stared at her face like he'd never seen her before. She did the same with him. The crisp morning air laden with Scotia moisture made breath visible.

Though Peyton Innes hadn't been told why he

had worked at least sixty-three miracles in a handful of days, or why he had driven the prince of Scotia to Aberdeen early that morning to wait by a brand new checked out, tricked out, fueled up, and ready to go airplane, he now had the key to the mystery.

Even a thickskulled old rugby player could recognize the look of mates kept apart. But why would that cause his future king to dissolve into a reckless mess? Pizza in the rain! With tour guides no less!

At that Aelsong opened up her beautiful mouth and said, "Duffy" so softly, but not softly enough that Innes didn't hear the Irish accent.

The expression on Innes face was truly horrified. His naturally ruddy complexion turned a little purple. When he could speak he said, "'Tis an elf, Duff! Set it away from ye, man!"

He said it as if he believed Aelsong Hawking to have a highly contagious and deadly disease. In his horrified state, Innes didn't see Elora come around the car moving so fast it was almost a flash, but he did know when he was taken firmly by the arm. Jerking his head to the side to see who would have the nerve to touch him in that manner, he came face to face with a pink-haired woman who stood nearly at eye level.

"Shhhh," she said. "Be quiet now. Please."

Innes tried to jerk his arm away. When he found it trapped in her grip, his eyes widened in surprise.

Duff angled his body toward them while keeping his arm around Song's shoulders. "Peyton, my friend, this is my mate, Aelsong Hawking."

Innes looked like he might faint. He swallowed hard. "Hawking?" he finally managed.

"Aye. She's exactly who you're thinkin' she is and understand this. I did no' choose her from a lineup of beautiful girls." He looked down at her. "Although I would've." She rewarded him with the dazzling Hawking smile he lived and breathed for. He pulled his gaze back to Innes. "And she did no' choose me. We're mated. You know what that means as well as I. Whate'er mysterious process put you with your Heather, the same paired me with Song.

"Perhaps there's a higher purpose at work. Certainly, in the dark hours, it has occurred to me. In the end though, I do no' know and 'tis no'my principal concern.

"I know 'tis damn inconvenient and likely to be more trouble than I can guess before 'tis done. But I would no' change it. The only thin' on Earth I'm sure of is that whatever bother comes, she's more than worth it."

Innes took in the way that Aelsong Hawking was looking at Duff Torquil and knew that the prince was right. It wasn't as if they were human. They didn't have a choice in the matter.

He looked at Elora. "Unhand me, woman."

Duff nodded toward Elora. "This is my solicitor, Peyton Innes. Peyton, this is my mate's sister-in-law, Elora Laiken Hawking. I suppose that means she is my sister-in-law by matin'."

She smiled. "Just Elora Laiken." She removed her hand from Innes' arm and offered it to him to shake instead. "How do you do, Mr. Innes?"

Innes looked at her hand reluctantly, but

finally shook. He lifted one brow. "You do no' sound like an elf."

"I am married to one though."

"Mmmmph."

Duff turned to Song. "Let's see what you brought. We need to finish loading and go."

"Is Mr. Innes our pilot?" Song asked looking at Innes warily.

Duff laughed and gave her a kiss on the cheek. "No, love. That would be me."

"Oh." She seemed delighted as she handed him the next bag. Song glanced over at Elora and some concern seemed to move across her features. She stood on tiptoe and said something in Duff's ear to which he nodded.

They were ready to go in minutes.

"Duff," Innes began, but the prince cut him off.

"You do no' need to worry about your involvement. Your fiduciary duty superseded all other concerns in this matter. No matter what comes of this, you're in the clear."

"I was no' goin' to say..." He looked at Aelsong. "If you need anythin', you can call."

Duff was clearly moved. He gripped Peyton by a shoulder. "Pey. Was no' expectin' that kindness. No' at all. Thank you."\

"Do no' be maudlin, little brother. 'Tis adventure ahead, aye?"

"Aye." Duff eyes crinkled around the edges with the sort of affection that ages like a patina over time. He felt Song pull at his sleeve. "Oh. One last thing. My new sister-in-law is practically a student driver and still learnin' right side rules at that. If you could manage to drive her and her little Vaux back to Charlotte Square safely, 'twould be much appreciated."

Innes looked from Elora to the silver Vauxhall. "Aye. It can be arranged."

Aelsong embraced Elora and put her cheek next to Elora's ear so she could whisper. "Sister, mine. Tell him why you did this and he'll no' be angry for long."

When Song pulled away, Elora asked, "Is that a guess, Song? Or a vision?"

The answer was a wink, a smile, and one more hug.

Elora stayed to watch the gleaming white plane taxi and take off. The mist had not only cleared, but given up for blue sky. She chose to take it as a sign.

She twirled the keys in her hand and turned to go, noticing that Innes was apparently engaged in some serious dialogue with a hangar employee. She started for the car, but was intercepted.

"Excuse me, Mrs. Hawking."

"Elora."

"As you please. His Highness, The Prince of Scotia Fae, has charged me with the honor of seein' you and your automobile safely to Charlotte Square. I have been licensed to operate vehicles in this country for a dozen years countin' and have no' a single crash to my name.

"Now, if you, madam, will oblige me with the keys, we shall undertake the journey south and I will endeavor to be pleasant company."

For a few beats she debated which might be worse, finding her way back to Headquarters via a seemingly endless series of bloody roundabouts or making conversation with Duff's stuffed shirt. She handed over the keys and got in the left hand side of the car, which meant that she was not driving.

As they left the airfield behind she turned to Innes. "Did you tell anyone?"

"Certainly no'."

"So you're not just Duff's lawyer?"

"He's close as can be with my younger brother. Watched him grow up." Elora nodded. "So. You're human, are ye?"

"More or less. Hybrid you might say."

"And you married an elf."

"I did."

"Well, there's no accountin' for taste."

"I've heard that."

When Duff settled on a plan that involved a getaway by private twin engine plane, he'd been thinking only in terms of logistics. It wasn't until they were at cruising speed that he realized that his beautiful new plane was more than a great escape. When it came to honeymoons, it was a stroke of genius. The close quarters of the cockpit and the cocoon environment of the plane made it feel like nothing existed except the two of them.

Song could not keep her eyes off him. Or her hands for that matter. Every few minutes she reached over to rearrange a lock of fine dark hair, not because it was out of place, but because she wanted the touch between her fingers.

Likewise, he was having a hard time believing that he was making away with a prize beyond measure and that any time he wanted he could look over and be zapped by electric blue eyes that had haunted him for more than a year.

Of course Song wanted to hear everything, how it had all come about, where they were going, what they were going to do, how long it would take to get there, and so on and so on. Since they had a little over two hours, he recalled as much detail as possible.

"So. Do you like strawberries?"

"To eat? Aye. To grow? 'Tis to be seen I suppose."

The weather stayed clear for their landing in the Faroe Islands. Duff was instrument rated, but nice weather is always nice and that's just a fact. The guest house had left word that they would send a car to pick them up and the wait wasn't long. Song pulled out a pink overnight bag while Duff grabbed a backpack and paid the hangar fee.

A fiftyish man picked them up in a Range Rover that had seen better days. As they got in the car Duff said, "Thank you for comin' for us. I'm Dougal and this is my wife, Shannon."

Song looked surprised, but said nothing. She realized that, while she had certainly had her bouts with celebrity and her rows with paparazzi, it was probably nothing compared to what Duff had been put through. This was, for all she knew, the first time in his life he'd ever experienced being out in the world without being recognized as *his Highness*.

A quick and surreptitious glance at his face confirmed that suspicion by virtue of the dreamy, contented expression he was wearing. She supposed it could be partly due to the fact that they were together, which warmed her all over.

The Faroes were everything he'd said. Breathtaking. Otherworldly. Like an outpost of the universe. The perfect place for a couple in self-imposed exile to spend a first night together.

They pulled off the road and drove toward the guest house, standing alone on a cliff and colorful as a Scandinavian book cover. The driver asked if they wouldn't like to stop in at the kitchen for a little warm lunch before they settle in at the cabin.

Duff looked at Song, who swallowed, remembering that she hadn't had breakfast. "Maybe just a bit of soup?"

He grinned down at her. "Have all the soup you want, Shannon."

After some hardy seafood bisque, they were shown to the cabin at the rear of the property. The hotelier had laid a nice fire while they had lunch and his wife had brought over a variety of sumptuous European-style snacks.

The cabin was understated, charming in a roughhewn sort of way. It had minimal bath facilities, but elegant white on white strip sheets on the bed, which the hotelier's wife had turned down as if she had anticipated their desire for a fireside nap.

Mr. Eskildsen set Aelsong's overnight bag down, said to enjoy their afternoon, to let him know if they needed anything, and mentioned that dinner would be around six.

After he left they stood staring at each other for a couple of minutes. A cloud cover had rolled in, graying up the day. The only light in the room was coming from the fire.

Duff had his backpack resting over one shoulder. He let it drop to the floor and pulled the zipper down the front of his jacket. Song's eyes followed the movement of the zipper like a lion watching a baby zebra wander away from its herd. He let the jacket drop on top of the backpack.

Her jacket fared a little better as it landed on the worn overstuffed leather chair that sat directly behind her thighs. Duff pulled off his ankle boots and dropped them. Song sat down in the chair to remove her Eskimo glugs. He pulled them off for her, which made her giggle. The giggle turned into a squeal when he picked her up out of the chair, wrapped her legs around his waist, and fell on the bed with her under him.

Duff looked down at Song smiling as his mouth touched hers and had just the briefest moment to experience the satisfaction of finally being with her before the fever took him, took them both.

The good-natured love play that led them to the bed turned serious the minute their bodies lined up with each other in full contact. Both of them had believed themselves to be sexually experienced, but neither had felt the hunger of channeling a gender's primal role at elemental force. Once ignited, the power surged into a control of its own.

They tore at each other's clothing and would

gladly have shredded it with their fingers had it given way. The natural progression of mating, denied for so long because of families and politics, took on an aberrant desperation that neither of them expected or were prepared for. They were both past the point, physically and emotionally, of touch being enough to ease the seasons of denial that had seemed to drag by endlessly. Their bodies had signaled recognition of mates and had punished their spirits for separation.

Now their bodies were in complete control and would be denied nothing. In an effort to cleave to each other and become one, they pulled hair and squeezed flesh with fingers. They clawed with nails and scraped with teeth. They cried from joy and from release and they cried in mourning for the time they'd been forced to spend apart.

It was not a violent coupling, an expression of need that transcends a human notion of marriage. It was survival. Mate or die.

Duff rode through the waves of three orgasms without pulling free of Song. One release was shortly followed by the crescendo of another arousal until all of their energy and most of the afternoon had been claimed. When their breathing began to even out, they rolled onto their sides facing each other, still sweat slicked, still entangled.

Song's hair was a mess of Medusa ringlets. Duff reached up and shoved a damp lock away from the side of her face and smiled.

She thought that the gray light of late afternoon coming through the high windows made his eyes look almost purple. They were mesmerizing. And they came with the dark fae that was hers. She traced the masculine line of his jaw with her fingertips. "Let's stay here forever and call it home."

He drew her in a fraction of an inch closer. "Where'er we're together from now on, 'tis home." She shivered and that action was met with a reaction of concern on his brow. "Do no' move. I'll be right back."

He rolled away and walked to the hearth, where the fire had all but died away. He stacked logs high enough to make it roar and as it began to rekindle he glanced over his shoulder and grinned.

"There. 'Twill be toasty in no time."

Leaning the poker against a stone edge, he turned to start back toward the bed, where he planned to crawl in for a renewed snuggle with his bride. Song had not pulled the covers over herself, but had, according to his instruction, stayed exactly as she was. When the prince turned and saw Aelsong's reclining nude form, he gasped and, for a heartbeat, froze at the sight.

He turned back to retrieve a candle from the mantel above the hearth and lit it with a kindling stick. When he reached the bed, he slowly ran the candle over Song's body from one end to the other, holding it aloft to hover inches above her skin for his close inspection.

"Fae's gods. Please tell me I did no' do this damage, beauty. 'Tis nothin' less than sacrilege."

"If you've desecrated my body, Duff Torquil, then find me guilty of the same crime. Just turn that bloody candle 'round on yerself."

He looked down, then withdrew the candle for a closer look at himself. After confirming that this body bore similar marks, scratches, bruises, and love bites, he looked up and laughed.

"Tore me up proper, did ye? Well, I'm glad to see you got your own licks in then."

He set the candle held in his right hand down on the bedside table while he absently rubbed his chest with his left hand and shook his head. Song's eyes were immediately drawn to the fact that his nipples pebbled with the contact.

"'Twas the furthest thin' I had in mind for the two of us to be doin' together today. I was thinkin' about a layover here in these tiny islands in the middle of the Iceland Sea and nothin' to do but spend a lazy afternoon beginnin' to learn about my mate." As his left hand had begun tracing a slow circular pattern on her thigh while he talked in soothing tones, her lips had parted further and further. His eyes ran up her body from the invisible circle he drew and stopped when they made contact with hers, which caused her breath to hitch. His brows furrowed into a scowl when he heard it. "You're no' afraid of me now, are you?"

Song stared at him with wide blue eyes. The Hawkings had a purely physical gift for hiding a world of sins behind a look that could easily be mistaken for innocence by someone who did not know them well. And Duff Torquil had a lot to learn about Aelsong.

She laughed in his face as she lunged at him and pinned him underneath her. "No' sure yet. Are you afraid of me?"

Looking up at her blinding smile, he could see the twinkle of mischief behind the illusion of dewy innocence. He knew he was looking at a woman that wouldn't frighten or cower easily. The Fates had given him a match. Someone to be with not merely because of the insistence of biological pairing, but someone he could love as well.

"Afraid of bein' without you. Ever again." He pulled her down into a kiss.

"What was it you say you had in mind that the two of us would be doin' together today?"

"Oh that." He grabbed her arms and rolled her under him so fast she swallowed a squeak. "'Tis better demonstrated than explained."

The prince of Scotia Fae proceeded to lovingly minister to each and every insult to his mate's body with tongue and kisses and sweet murmurs of love.

CHAPTER 7

Thursday night Storm and Litha carried on a silent conversation at dinner while Rosie intermittently pushed food around her plate. She hadn't really expected that Glen would respond to her ultimatum and, perhaps on some deep core level she might have known she wouldn't have respected him if he had.

In some ways, having been born with her parents' education and memories, Rosie was both knowledgeable and wise. In some ways though, she was as immature and inexperienced in how to manage life in the world as any twenty-year-old. She was too proud to admit that she'd made a mistake by proclaiming a high stakes, winner-take-all tug of war with Glen over *his* career choice, didn't know how to admit that she'd been wrong and back away from her actions, so she'd determined that she was going to dig herself further into the sinkhole.

Rosie put the fork down and sat back. She looked between the two other people at the table, closer to the physical age of peers than parents. Her eyes flicked to the clock one more time.

"I have something to tell you. I need to go away for a little bit."

"What do you mean 'away'?" Storm hadn't wasted any time slipping comfortably into the role of father and nothing about the unusual character of their situation seemed to deter him.

"I mean I'm going to take a break from what I'm doing."

Storm choked out a laugh. "Take a break from what you're doing? And what is that? You aren't doing anything."

"Storm!" Litha's tone was full of reproof.

"Well, it's true, isn't it?"

Litha stared at him, angry because she was afraid he was hurting Rosie's feelings and wanting very badly to be able to argue the point. The fact that he was right didn't make him more endearing at that moment. Sometimes being consistently right was his most infuriating quality. This was one of those times.

Oddly they really had never gotten around to discussing what Rosie might *do* with her time. In the beginning every day of her existence was a new miracle, right up until those daily miracles were overshadowed by a missing father and a look-alike under house arrest. While everybody was thinking in terms of hour to hour, everybody forgot to talk to Rosie about what she intended to do with her splendid array of abilities and inconceivable list of possibilities.

Rosie wasn't accustomed to the challenging accusation of paternal disappointment and had flushed pink in the face, either from anger or embarrassment or humiliation. It was impossible to tell.

Storm narrowed his eyes. "Does this have something to do with Glen?"

Rosie's eyes jerked to Storm's so quickly that she might as well have shouted yes. "Glen is no longer part of the picture where I'm concerned.

Anyway, as I was saying, I'm going to be gone for a while. You're not to worry." She looked at Litha. "If there's an emergency, Lally will be able to find me."

She kissed Litha on the cheek and gave her a hug. Litha looked a little stunned, but patted her forearm and stroked her hair once, twice. Rosie approached her dad, who sat stiffly. She bent to kiss his cheek and hug him in the same manner. When she put her arms around his shoulders, he melted. He pushed back the chair, stood and put his arms around her.

"Do I need to kick his ass?"

She put her arms around his waist and shook her head. With her cheek against his chest, she said, "No. You went right to the heart of the problem. All I want to do is be with Glen and I tried to force him to feel the same way about me. Maybe, if I spend a little time away... Maybe I need to think about doing something myself. I love you, Dad."

"I love you, Rosie."

And she was gone.

As Storm's empty arms dropped to his sides his mind presented him with a snapshot it had taken on a day when he'd been fourteen years old. He was in the car with Sol, pulling away from his parents' house. They stood together in the shallow front yard holding hands and watched him drive away. His limited post-pubescent understanding had registered the look on his mother's face as sadness, the sort that would be forgotten by the time she reached the kitchen and started thinking about what to make for dinner.

Now he knew that look wasn't something so inconsequential as sadness. It was the face of loss as devastating as the discovery of a missing limb. He made a vow to himself that he would replace the years his mother lost with time and attention. Never too late.

He turned to Litha as his mind replayed part of the earlier conversation. "Who's Lally?"

Rosie had waited on a tabletop boulder on a windswept mountaintop of Prescient Dimension where she went when she needed to contact Kellareal for longer than usual. She explained that she wanted a change of environment, where she could take a break from her life and rethink the direction of things.

She knew she'd pushed things with Glen, but she also knew that, despite her feelings and desires to the contrary, the relationship wasn't serious and wasn't going to be. Not for a while. He'd made his decision. He was going wherever Z Team went and at least she had enough pride to know she wasn't going to follow along like a camp whore. Even if he'd let her. Which he probably wouldn't.

So she'd take a lesson from that and maybe look for a little adventure of her own while she was young. *While she was young.*

The breeze that blew her wild hair back from her face grew a little softer. Kellareal appeared to float down from the sky wearing a long white robe that billowed around him, arms outstretched as if inviting embrace, and landed in front of her soundlessly. She knew he would want to be congratulated on the theater, so she clapped. He bowed.

"Lally. How long do you think I'm going to live?"

"You called me for that?" He picked up a pebble, sat down beside her, and threw it out over the canyon overlook. "We may have to rethink your summoning privilege if you're going to abuse it, young lady."

"No, that's not why I called, but since you're here..."

"Well, your elemental side is very long lived, meaning eons. Your human side is cursed with short life under the best of circumstances. Then there is the issue of fragility, the moment to moment uncertainty, the... risk, if you will, of being human. I tell you, it causes me to marvel constantly at their courage. Living under those circumstances, I'm not sure that I wouldn't just curl into a ball and hope for sudden death to put an end to the suspense."

"If they only knew how cynical real angels sound, you would never get your own TV shows."

"Hmmm. No doubt." He grinned. "But a few feather sightings would bring them right back around."

Rosie giggled. "You're hopeless."

"And is *that* why you wanted to see me?"

"No. I need to get out of town for a while, change of scenery. Maybe I need to broaden my experience."

"Get out of town," he repeated drily. "What does your mother think of this?"

"She thinks she can get in touch with you if

there's an emergency and that you'll know where to find me."

The angel pursed his lips, stood and paced for a while. "Vacations are fun. Sabbaticals are informative. Quests are enlightening, sometimes cathartic. Retreats are rejuvenating. Treks are adventurous. This?" He stopped and looked at Rosie. "This sounds like running away. Hard to put a noble spin on running away."

"I'm not necessarily asking for your blessing, Lally. Just a place to…"

"…hide?"

Rosie flushed. "It's a favor."

Kellareal looked at her for a long time. "I can't decide without hearing the whole story. I want to know exactly what it is you're running from and what you're hoping to gain."

By the time Rosie finished spelling it out, she was sorry she had started the whole thing. Spelling out what had brought her to that mountaintop sounded spoiled, selfish, childish and silly, even to herself as she said it. She supposed that was one of the angel's goals in having her connect the dots out loud. She hoped that the worst of it, humiliation-wise, was over.

"Have you thought about how long you want to be away?"

She hadn't thought about it.

"Do I have to decide that now?"

"No. I suppose you can do a pay-as-you-go plan."

"Wait. What do you mean pay-as-you-go?"

The angel took her elbow and pulled her to her feet. Standing several inches taller, he looked down into her face. "You're right, Elora Rose. It is time for you to learn something of the world. First lesson, nothing's free."

A few minutes later they were standing on the periphery of an enclosure – a crude, gray stone wall. From what Rosie could see, there were homes and buildings built around a park-like commons area with sparse gas lighting, but the overall impression of the place was of a fort. Through a break in the wall that formed a gate with iron bars, she could see that they were on a hilltop overlooking the lights of a large town.

The air was scented with the welcoming smell of wood burning fires releasing white smoke into the atmosphere. The prominent feature of the compound was a long row of motorcycles, some of which had parts shiny enough to reflect in the cold moonlight.

"Where are we?" Rosie asked.

"It's a project of mine, Rosie. A secret. You can't ever tell anyone."

"Okay."

"Promise."

"I do."

"They're what's left of Telstar."

"Telstar? Isn't that one of those worlds that went crazy with genetic engineering?"

"I guess it depends on what you mean by 'went crazy'."

"Okay. Let me put it this way. You start out with a wolf. You end up with a **Shih Tzu** or a Pug.

You start out with a human, you end up with a ..."

"The flaw in your argument is the owners of dogs like that would say they're an improvement on the prototype."

Rosie blinked. "So you're saying you're taking me to a place where I should be prepared for…" She left the end of that sentence for him to fill in the blank.

"Okay. Consider this your briefing in a nutshell. There were some experiments that went on for a couple of generations. People became concerned and even invoked religious invective to fuel a movement to eradicate all the produce of the experiment."

"Produce?" He nodded. "You mean the people?"

"That is what I mean and I, ah, intervened. I saw an opportunity to solve two problems. There was a group of people here in need of protection, which is one of the ways Telstar skills might be used. This group was under threat of genocide. I knew the Telstar survivors would relate. So I paired them with the humans that needed them. "

He waved his hand at the darkness. "It's pretty here. This dimension hasn't been ruined yet. Lots of everything. Gives them a chance." He looked at Rosie. "You know?"

"Wasn't that against some rule?"

The angel pursed his lips and heaved a big sigh. "Rules need to be placed in the context of knowing the rule makers. And their agenda."

Rosie studied his face in the darkness. "Lally, you're an anarchist."

"Guess that depends on who you talk to."

"Are there others?"

"Other elementals who think like I do?" She nodded. "Yeah. Anyway. They've been here for a while now. Some have started families. Their own take on culture is starting to emerge. Interesting to watch. The one in charge of the place is a nice fellow with a nice family. Owes me a favor. Simple as that."

"Does everybody in the multiverse owe you a favor?"

His mouth twitched at the corner as he looked down at her. "Working on it." His eyes drifted back to the settlement. Rosie thought she saw a hint of pride. Proud sponsor perhaps.

"This could be a good place to get your thoughts sorted out. They'll give you a job and who knows? Maybe a new perspective. So welcome to the EC. That's what they call it, short for Exile Camp. By the way, don't mention Telstar. They don't like to be reminded. I don't blame them. They left that behind to start a new life." He turned to face Rosie. "A new world really."

She looked around again. "What's with the motorcycles?"

His expression was definitely sheepish. "Oh, they, the Telstar, like them. A lot. So they became part of our arrangement. I made an adjustment to the engines so they'll run on water and threw tools and maintenance stuff in with the deal."

"Are you saying that they're weren't motorcycles here before?"

"No. Every dimension develops differently. You know that."

Victoria Danann

"Well, yes… So how did you get motorcycles here?"

He laughed. "Rode them."

"You did not."

He nodded, grinning. "One at a time."

"I didn't know you could ride a motorcycle through the passes."

"For all I know, I'm the only one who knows it. Let's keep it that way. Okay?"

She shrugged. "Okay. What do they look like?"

"Look like?" Kellareal laughed out loud. "Oh, sweet baby."

154

CHAPTER 8

Song and Duff hopped along the route he had mapped out. They had lots of time to collapse a courtship into a matter of days, alone together in the cab of a private aircraft that would seat four, but felt perfect for two. They told each other their favorite autobiographical stories, their likes and dislikes, their opinions about everything from politics and ecology and economy to kilts and food. Song tried to carefully recall every detail of Glen's account of the division of the Dana people into elves and fae so that she could repeat it close to verbatim.

They were held over at the Igaluit outpost for an extra day because of bad weather, but they spent the day in bed and were glad of it. Since they had made it to the Northwest Territories and were officially under the protection of the Canadian government, they shed a world of stress and smothered each other in the carefree regard that mates normally share with partners.

They would be surprising the world with their announcement on the fifth day of their elopement. When they arrived in Quebec, a crowd of reporters was waiting along with a full security team to escort them to the Fairmont Le Chateau Frontenac where they would give a joint press conference with the

Prime Minister and then spend a day enjoying the oldest city in North America.

Elora had finished her afternoon class and was looking forward to spending the rest of the day with her boys. She turned the key to the apartment and was overwhelmed by the marvelous smell. Ram must have decided to cook something wicked spicy for dinner. The TV on the kitchen bar was turned on, but Ram wasn't in sight. He must have been watching while he cooked.

She stepped over to the stove and stirred flanked steak pieces with poblano peppers and she wasn't sure what all else was in there.

Ram came walking out of the bedroom saying something into the phone. He looked up at her with eyes gone dark just as he was saying goodbye and closed the phone. She could tell from a mile away that something was way off.

"What's wrong, Ram?"

He came around the bar slowly and stood over the stove. "That was Dougherty. Remember him? Orderly from Edinburgh?"

Elora shook her head. "No. Why?"

"Works in the clinic. I got to know him when Helm was born, while you were recoverin' from hypothermia."

"Oh. Doesn't ring a bell."

"Strangest fuckin' thin'." Ram gave the colorful concoction a stir, turned the heat down to low, and faced Elora leaning back against a counter. "He says he saw you in Edinburgh last Thursday.

Says some fella drove you right up to Charlotte Square. Says you got out, said goodbye, got back in the car and drove it under the Headquarters buildin' to the garage. Says the 'gentleman' walked off t'other way." Ram's nostrils flared just a little when he punctuated the word 'gentleman' with air quotes.

He paused while he studied Elora's reaction. "Said this was a nice lookin', well-dressed, fae fella about your age, sandy hair, couple a inches over six feet. Course I would have liked to tell him he was sorely mistaken, but there's no one looks like you, to be sure.

"So tell me. This sudden shoppin' trip to London you were needin' so badly because of the strain of the baby and the battle and so forth." He looked around for dramatic effect. "Where are the packages?"

"Ram," Elora began quietly, cautiously because she could see he was a lit fuse. "You can *not* be suggesting what I think you're suggesting. I'm elf. Mated to you and utterly incapable of what I think you're suggesting."

"Elf. Well, you're… what was that? Ninety-six percent? Ninety-eight percent? Maybe the other missin' percents are doin' somethin' besides roundin' the points of ears." She winced a little at that. "All I know is that you told me you were shoppin' in fuckin' London with my best friend's wife while you were in fuckin' fairyland doin' what?" He paused for a breath thinking he could get control, but failed. His eyes flashed. "WHERE. ARE THE. PACKAGES?"

"Being shipped. You know you can't lug packages through the passes."

Ram searched her eyes and grew quiet. "Please tell me that's no' all you have to say to me."

Just as Elora opened her mouth, their attention was jerked away from the conversation by hearing a familiar name on the bar TV that had been left on. Princess Aelsong Hawking.

When Ram turned and saw his sister sitting in between the Prime Minister of Canada and the fae prince, his jaw went slack and the color began to drain from his face. The Prime Minister was speaking.

"Prince Torquil and Princess Hawking are a couple. They formally applied for political asylum and it has been granted. They hope that their families, their governments, and their people will accept them, but if that doesn't happen, they're prepared to become Canadian citizens."

Ram's knees bent. He sank downward until he was sitting on the floor. "My sister is a traitor."

"Ram!" Elora gaped at him.

He moved his face toward her, but was looking through eyes that were dazes and unfocused. "My sister is a traitor. My mate is no' faithful. How can these thin's be?"

"Rammel. You need to snap out of it. Neither one of those things is true."

The unfocused look in Ram's eyes seemed to clear just a little as he repeated, "No' true."

As she watched, the haze then dissipated quickly and was replaced with a sharpness that was too sudden for comfort. He pinned Elora with a look.

"No. 'Tis no' true, is it? You were no' with that bugger because you were bein' unfaithful to me.

You were there because you were helpin' them!"

He exploded to his feet. For a moment Elora thought he might try to throttle her. She'd never seen him so angry. Then she remembered what Song had whispered right before she'd flown away.

Elora reached out to touch him, but he stepped back.

"Ram," she said softly, "Tell me something. Did you choose me?"

His brows drew together. "What?"

"Did you choose me to be your mate?"

His brows snapped together. "What in Paddy's name does that…?"

"It has everything to do with this," she interrupted. "Answer. Did. You. Choose. Me."

He crossed his arms over his chest and stared for a few beats with his scowl firmly in place. Finally he said, "No."

Elora nodded. She said nothing more, but watched the lines smooth away from his brow as the profound truth of that gradually sank in.

"I did no', but it *feels* like I did."

"It's the same for me. I don't know what love is. I don't know where it comes from or where it goes. I only know it's what I feel for you. And if somebody took you away from me, I would die. That's not drama. It's not exaggeration. It's just a fact." Ram stared. "So do you know what I'm going to say next?"

"Aye. You're goin' to say, 'What if I was fae?'"

"Yeah. What if?'

He slowly closed the three steps between them

and pressed her so close she could barely think.

"Nothin' could stop me. No' so long as I had breath."

She put her face in his neck and inhaled the comfort of his scent, musk and wild fern. "Do you know what I'm going to say next?"

"Aye. You're goin' to say she's my sister and I should bloody well be on her side."

"And what will you say to that?"

He looked down and to the side. "I do no' think I have any choice but to agree. My wife has an invisible, but permanent grip on my balls." For that she blew a raspberry into the skin of his neck that she'd been nuzzling a moment before. "So you say, but 'tis a shit storm the size of Ireland and Scotia combined. And I *am* just one elf. "

She had to chuckle at that. "Humility's not a good fit for you, Rammel."

"No' tryin' to be cute. Elves are stubborn. Fae are pissy and unreasonable. Sortin' this out, well, 'tis goin' to take more good intentions."

"It's a good thing we have an inside man at the Irish royal house." She squeezed his buttocks with both hands then looked around. "Where's Helm?"

Coupling the action with the question, his grin turned lascivious. "Elsbeth's. Entertainin' Finn." That revelation was punctuated with a well-placed tongue at the base of her throat and fingers that worked their way inside the waist band of her pants so that he could give her a return squeeze hand to cheek.

"How about this for a plan? You make sweet love to me to show me how you're never going to doubt me again because, whatever those mystery percents are doing, they belong to you and only you and you know that all the way down to your beautifully formed toes. Then you can feed me yummy, spicy dinner while I tell you a story about your ancestors."

He smiled as he continued nuzzling her neck. "You like my toes?"

Elora was thinking about whether or not to answer honestly when Ram's phone rang. He paid no attention. He was on a mission working a path of alternating nuzzles, kisses and licks. Without thinking about it she glanced down at the bar and saw that it was his mother calling.

"It's your mother."

Ram stopped like a freeze frame, but only for a fraction of a second. "Ignore it," he said in a raspy voice.

She wanted to do exactly that, badly, but she pulled back instead. "Any other time. But I can't. You can't." She picked up the phone and handed it to him.

His shoulders slumped, but he took it looking resigned. "Mum." Pause. "Mum" Pause. "Mum." He looked up at Elora with big pleading eyes. "Mum, I can no' understand with you cryin' like that."

After the press conference, the Prime Minister lingered for a private meeting with her country's two newest celebrity guests to ask about their plans. The woman did not relax just because everyone else had left the room. Aelsong may have found the experience remarkable, possibly harrowing, but the head of the Canadian government took it in stride.

"I am principle holder in a Canadian corporation that owns a lovely property east of Prince George. We plan to live there for now."

Madame Minister's facial expression was a pleasant mask that gave away nothing, but she raised a brow slightly at that. "I see. What are your plans for security?"

Duff was clearly not prepared for that question. "We did no' make plans for security. We wish to live as private individuals, no' as public or political figures."

She stared for a couple of beats before smiling in a way that almost looked like she felt pity for them. "If wishes were fishes."

Duff looked at Song, who shook her head slightly. "Pardon?"

She took in a deep breath. "You must know that, while this is all very romantic, it's also made a lot of people very, very angry. I can't welcome you into my country and not give you any protection. If something happens to you here, how do you think that would make me look?"

"Honestly, I had no' thought about how it would make you look."

"Clearly not. Young people are always thinking only about themselves." She shook her head briskly as if intending to appear firm. "No. Security is a mandate and, obviously, it shouldn't be a financial burden on the Canadian people. So you need it and you need to pay for it."

Duff stared at the Prime Minister. "It would have been very helpful if you'd mentioned this before today." She shrugged. "So how much security is bein' mandated?"

At the wave of a hand to the guard just inside the door, he opened for a suited man carrying a file. He walked briskly, with great economy of movement, to the oval table sitting at the end of the room inside a giant bay window. The Prime Minister nodded toward a chair next to her. He sat and laid the file on the table in front of him.

Duff's gaze focused on the file, wondering what it might contain.

"Prince Torquil, Princess Hawking, this is Mr. Brachen from the CNS. He will be supervising your case and insuring that your security needs are met so that there are no unfortunate incidents while you're here."

The prince was unconsciously holding Song's hand tighter than he would have intended as he felt his dream of living a quiet remote life with his mate slipping through his fingers like sand.

"Now, if you'll excuse me, I have to get back to Ottawa. So nice to have met you." She smiled at Aelsong. "And welcome to Canada!"

She swooped toward the door as if it would open magically before she arrived at the threshold. And it did.

Mr. Brachen cleared his throat. "Well, as has been said, welcome to Canada."

Duff and Song, both feeling more apprehensive with each passing minute, more like prisoners than refugees, murmured polite thank yous.

"The thin' is, Mr. Brachen. We were plannin' to ease our way into the livin' of a remote life, be reclusive until people in the area got used to us. We do no' have accommodation for others. Nor is there accommodation nearby."

Brachen nodded. "I understand. Perhaps we can find a way for the Prime Minster to feel reasonably *secure*," he smiled at the emphasized word like it was a private joke used often in his line of work, "without completely dismantling your vision. In other words," he looked between the two of them, "compromise."

"Well, Mr. Brachen, that may depend partly on my mate's inclination to agree with your proposal and partly on how much compromise I can afford."

"Fair enough. Let's find a starting point, shall we?"

"Very well, For starters, is there any way around this... mandate?"

Brachen raised his chin, closed the file, and folded his hands together. "You could refuse, but you'd need to make a formal statement to that effect, which would make you vulnerable to any lunatic who could figure out where you are – not that hard to do," he said under his breath, "and," he smirked, "elves and fae are given to lunacy even when unprovoked. You two have poked the rabid dog with a stick until he's now howling looney tunes."

Duff looked down at his hands. The picture of living with Song by that mountain stream had been so vivid, so perfectly clear. He saw a beautiful feminine hand come into his field of vision and close over his own clasped hands, and there it was. Even in the midst of bitter disappointment, he wasn't alone anymore. It wasn't about the house in BC. It was about Aelsong Hawking. She was his home wherever she was.

He looked up into her face and without looking away said, "Mr. Brachen, I've no' had a chance to speak with my bride since learnin' there's a stump in the path. Would you be so kind as to give us a minute to ourselves?"

They heard the chair move back. "Certainly. Just let the guard outside the door know when you're ready to resume our discussion. Or if you'd like your refreshments refreshed."

Song had spent the past year diligently exercising mind over a body in mating heat, which meant that its entire purpose for existence was finding Duff Torquil and coupling with him. He was the other half of their biological whole and, what she needed more than anything was to be with him. But that was not the same thing, as spending time with a person and coming to appreciate the subtle way he looks askance when he's uncertain or the way his lashes linger on his cheek when he's summoning patience.

She may have only spent a week with him, but she knew him well enough to read the disappointment that was radiating off of him in waves. His dream had just been shattered. For her, she didn't particularly care for remote mountain living. She could like it or not, but she didn't like to see what she was seeing on her mate.

"So, Dougal," she said brightly. She got a little smile in response to her use of the a.k.a. "We're hittin' our first bump. I'm told life is full of them. We'll just be takin' a step back, seein' where we are, makin' a new plan and startin' off again."

He reached up, touched her cheek, and sighed deeply. "I was so sure this was good, I did no' come up with a Plan B."

"It was good. It is good. Let's hear what Word Game has to say. Maybe it will no' be so bad as you're thinkin'. Aye?"

"Do no' really see another option."

"So we ride along until we do."

Duff nodded. "So you're smart, too?"

"Tcha. Landed ENT's sexiest man alive, did I no'?

That earned her a hearty laugh with resplendent twinkling eyes.

CHAPTER 9

Over the next day Duff hammered out something with Brachen that he thought was feasible with his means. They would be accompanied to Prince George and would be met there by the small security force that had been handpicked to insure their safety. They would erect temporary quarters until the property could be turned into a "compound".

When the agreement was struck, Song and Duff were eager to get out of the hotel and resume their journey toward their new life. They sat close together in the back of the SUV that was transporting them to the airport where they were expecting a gauntlet of reporters.

As they were hurried along by security people and jostled inside the lounge of one of the private jet hangars, they were separated and, before either knew what was happening, they were wearing handcuffs and pushed through doors on opposite sides of the room.

The two large elves who had custody of Song weren't prepared for a demonstration of Hawking fire. She not only broke free, but managed to knock one of them down. Just inside the door to the adjacent hangar, Duff was engaged in his own skirmish with well-trained people who had been better prepared for resistance.

She was overtaken before she reached him, but not before being forced to witness him being tasered. She would spend the rest of her life wishing she could purge that sight from her memory, for all the good that would do.

The press was waiting en masse outside the palace gates at Derry hoping to get photos of Aelsong Hawking being formally extradited on a convenient technicality and forced back home by the king. The palace guards held the crowd back while the caravan with dark tint window drove through. The cars made their way to the rear entrance at garden level so that no photo ops would be possible.

The guards who had been charged with the duty of delivering the princess escorted Song into one of the small parlors used by the family. Her parents were waiting along with her brother who stood looking officious by a cheery, popping fire.

After the escorts removed the handcuffs, Aelsblood nodded and they withdrew closing the door behind them.

"Welcome back, sister." She said nothing, didn't even bother to change expression. She simply turned and started for the door. "You'll be findin' a suitable complement of security staff on the other side of the door to insure that you do no' get lost and temporarily lose touch again."

She turned around slowly. "You plan to keep me prisoner, do you?"

Tepring began crying softly. "Truly. 'Tis the safest thin' for you. Your behavior is thought to be traitorous no' just to your family, but to your entire species."

Aelsong turned to her father. "What have you to say about this, Da?"

Aelsblood answered before their father. "For gods' sake, Song. He's fae!"

Song ignored that and waited for Ethelred's answer. He met his daughter's gaze without censure or recrimination, nor did he convey that she would find support there either. He gave the subtlest of shrugs and said in a tone that sounded casual against the backdrop of his wife's weeping, "He's the king."

While Aelsong stared at her father, trying to read what was there, she heard Aelsblood say, "Go to your rooms, Song. You need, what do they call it? Oh yes, a time out."

Song blinked and turned slowly. She walked back toward the fire where her brother stood. The large, ancient bit of firetending equipment caught her eye.

If there was anything worse than having one's other half forcibly ripped away and tortured in front of them, it was having one's sibling behave as if she was an adolescent caught at a prank. She swept up the heavy iron poker and, brandishing it with two hands, took a swipe that looked like a worthy attempt at beheading her brother.

In a defensive move that probably saved Song from execution for the crime of assassinating the monarch, he threw his forearm up and blocked the blow at the last second, yelling, "Ow," and "Guards," in rapid succession. "You've probably broke my arm, you nitwit. Are you thinkin' you have no' done enough damage for now? You know what we used to do with elves who committed treason? We did no' lock them in their girly sweet rooms."

The guards were awaiting instructions. "Take her to her rooms. Lock her in. Post a guard outside and make sure she does no' leave. Be very certain that she does no' get messages in or out either."

As the guards were trying to drag her out, Song had a few choice parting remarks for Aelsblood that reminded all the household staff within hearing distance of another of her brothers. "Lock me in, will you? You'd better make sure I ne'er get out. If I e'er do, I *will* kill you next time, you bloody cocksuckin' source of pus and piss. Do you know why you do no' know how it feels to be mated? Because the mysteries decided there's *no* female elf, no matter how horrid, who should be so accursed."

"Get her out of here," Aelsblood said, holding his arm.

As soon as they were gone, Tepring rose from the sofa having said not one word. On the way out of the room, she stopped in front of her son and slapped him on the neck with the hand that wasn't holding a handkerchief.

"Mum! For… what in Paddy's name is that about? Has the entire palace gone mad?"

He looked over at his father who was glaring at him. It was a look he had often seen trained on Ram when he was growing up, but he had never experienced the full impact of the old man's formidable personality directed straight at him. It was very uncomfortable.

"Did it no' occur to you that perhaps we should talk about what has happened as a family?"

Aelsblood looked confused. "Well, no. What

do you mean?"

"Do you see this incident purely as a matter of state? That's certainly the impression you just gave your mother and your sister."

"As a member of the royal family my sister has a special obligation to…"

"I believe what you missed in your analysis of this situation is that the key to that sentence was family. Your mother would have liked to see you treat Aelsong with love and sympathy. You did no' even manage to squeak out respect. It was shameful."

Aelsblood gaped. "Unbelievable. My sister runs away with the heir to our enemy's throne and you sit here callin' my behavior shameful."

The former king sighed deeply and looked at the rich amber color of the whiskey in the tumbler he held in his hand. "I wonder where this whiskey came from."

"'Tis Lagavulin,"

"Aye. Well, no one can say the fae are without worth then."

A similar scene was taking place some hundred and fifty miles northeast, as the raven flies, across the channel of the Irish Sea. The fae king lectured his son for an hour about the way the "escapade" had turned a well-ordered society into an uproar, about how he was a failure as a son and heir to the throne and about how the beloved son of the fae people would now probably have bottles and garbage thrown at him if he tried to go outside the palace gates. Duff's mother never said a word, but reached now and then to smooth away a tear.

Duff would have been happy to go toe to toe with his father if it would serve any purpose or be productive in any way. For the time being, he knew the only thing he could do was to pretend to be compliant and wait for another chance to escape.

Grieve stood, as the prince was led past him, but didn't look up and meet his eyes. When the doors of his quarters closed behind him, Duff looked around his room. No way to get a message to Song. He wondered what was happening to her and hoped to the gods that her people were blaming him and not her. He would never forget the look on her face as she was being pulled away.

For a long time he simply stood in his room, not being able to summon the motivation to move. When it got dark, he decided to take off his coat. As he did, he caught a whiff of her scent where she'd been leaning against him in the car on the way to the airport in Quebec. Wondering how old a twenty-five-year-old could feel, he lay down on top of his bed with the sleeve of that coat close to his face.

"They've got her confined to quarters in a house arrest sort of situation. She will no' eat anythin' and will no' even talk to our mum."

Elora was shaking her head and looking dumbstruck. "And that reaction comes as a surprise to a species that mates for life? What other result could they possibly expect?"

Ram shrugged. "They were probably in denial about the possibility of a true matin', believin' us to be different species and all."

Elora exhaled an exasperated breath. "So it's going to take the death of a royal couple, children of enemies, to prove that you're the same?" Saying that out loud caused Elora to catch her breath. "Ram, the odds of that, I mean the odds against that would have to be impossible. It almost sounds like divine intervention, doesn't it? Like some cosmic force stepping in."

"I wish 'twas one of your stories, Elora, but 'tis only a tragic coincidence."

"Will they let you see her?"

"I suppose I could if I was there. Unless my brother is attemptin' to top the record he currently holds for world's biggest asshole by far. Why? What are you thinkin'?"

"Let me get back to you on that. I'm going to lay it out for Litha and ask if she can think of anything."

Ram glanced at his watch. "Could no' hurt. How much does she know?"

"Nothing."

He raised a brow. "So she *really* thought you were goin' shoppin'."

"Don't sound so cynical. Yes. Well, I mean, she thought there might be more to it, but accepted when I declined to elaborate."

"So, in other words, she's as scared of you as I am."

"Uh-huh." Elora moved her head from side to

side. "Go make your call."

"I see now why you didn't want to answer my questions."

Litha had listened to the entire story from the beginning, "...the night we took Kay's sisters out pubbing in Edinburgh. They met just about an hour before you accidentally burned the place down," to the end, "Now they're both political prisoners. Song's not eating. We don't know how Duff is, but I fear that he's the same.

"So the question is, with all your vast knowledge and practically limitless resources..."

"Elora."

"Okay, just saying, can you think of anything?"

"Think of anything? Spell it out. I'm not sure what you mean."

"Is there anything we can do for them?" There was a long enough pause on the other end of the conversation to finally make Elora prompt to be sure she wasn't alone on the line. "Litha?"

"I'm running some scenarios, trying to find a possibility. Let's just say that, for the sake of argument, there was something..."

"What's the deal?"

"Hmmm. Got something in mind."

"In the words of great women, spell it out."

Litha shared the high points of Rosie's getaway. "I was just thinking that, if my friend should find out that she'd like someone to talk to, you know, she's always listened to you."

"Ha!"

"Well, she hasn't always done what you advised, but she did always listen."

"Fair enough. And, yes, of course. You don't need to call in a favor for that, Litha. And you know it."

"I have obligations to uphold as a card carrying part demon, Elora."

"So are you going to tell me what you're thinking?"

"Got to make a call first."

"Like a phone call or like a witchy kind of call?"

Litha started laughing. "I'll let you know something soon as I hear back."

"When?"

"Have you always been this pushy?"

"I guess I'm a sucker for love. And eating."

"Yeah. Me, too. I'll hurry. Promise."

Litha waited patiently at Kellareal's summoning spot. If there was a bell or a buzzer, she'd have been sitting on it in an obnoxious way. As it was, the same thing could be accomplished telepathically.

"Alright. Alright. Is there a fire?" He smiled. "Get it, Firestarter."

"I do. You're one of my funniest friends."

"They why aren't you laughing?"

"Because I need your help. I want to take an

elf and a fae off world and hide them, give them sanctuary."

"Why? What's wrong?"

Litha summed up the story with all the pertinent details.

"Usually there wouldn't be anything, but there may be a loophole."

"Oh?"

The angel's lips tightened. "Council business." He looked at Litha like he'd made up his mind about something. "Let me plead the case. I'll find you as soon as I have an answer. Cross your fingers."

CHAPTER 10

"The Enforcer's here."

"What does he want?"

"Well, I don't know that, do I? That's why he's here. To tell us. Right?"

"Do you always have to be so smarmy? You might know because you asked. Right?"

"Oh. For crap's sake, let him in."

"S'up, angel?" asked Hu.

"If your graces would indulge me, I'd like to ask for a guideline waiver. A young couple in Loti Dimension in need of sanctuary."

"Loti Dimension?" Culain looked up.

"Yes. Of all things the prince of fae and princess of elves are a mated couple whose families have separated and imprisoned them because of an historical misunderstanding."

"You see?" said Ming Xia. "Culain's children are *always* getting into trouble. I told you it would be a mistake to interfere. All we had to do was remain detached," he looked at Heralda pointedly, "and objective and let them die out, which is what a strain ruled by passions is supposed to do."

"Kill each other off you mean," said Rager drily.

"What's the difference?" Ming then changed to a falsetto tone to mock Culain, even though Culain didn't have a high singsong voice. "I'll give them arts

– song, dance, and storytelling to use as an outlet for their passions so that it isn't always expressed in war or lust." He switched back to his normal voice. "Then when that didn't work out, you got witch girl to meddle with the genetics so that they're monogamous and mate for life. You thought then they'd stop killing each other over women."

"And they did, didn't they?" said Heralda. "So why don't you mind your own fucking business. Go back to your sudoku."

"Since when is Council business not my fucking business, Gothmerelda?" Theasophie drew air through her teeth when she turned over the next tarot card in the spread she was reading. "Every time we muck around stuff goes further off track and you know that. Look at this very thing. You introduced a new code to the genetics to spark the instinct toward mating and it was that very thing that almost ended the entire race when those twins were born and both of them wanted the same girl. Isn't it ironic?"

"Ming's just jealous because he doesn't have any children," said Heralda.

He gaped. " JEALOUS?!? Look at the muddle your vampire have caused. I thank atoms every day that I *don't* have children."

"Where's Etana?" asked Hu. Culain, Heralda, and Minq all looked at him. "What!"

"We all agreed when we started that if any of our hobby projects started to get out of control that we would take steps to insure that no individual interest threatened the group assignment. We don't want to be stuck here forever, you know," Ming continued even though no one was paying attention.

"How long do you think it's been since she was here?" Heralda cocked her head to the side and challenged Huber Quizno with a borderline sneer.

"It's been a long time. I know that. I'm just saying that maybe it's time someone questioned where she is. Don't you think? I mean in Earth terms it's probably been…"

"…two thousand years," said Ming.

"There! Two thousand years!"

Heralda shook her head. "That's not very long, Hu. She can't stand to be around us because…"

Hu took his cue and made the turkey gobbling noise that he did so well which had become their private code for the constant in-Council squabbling.

"Exactly. You know she's flitting from dimension to dimension trying to start peace movements." Heralda laughed and shook her head. "She kills me. She was probably Cervantes' muse."

Culain flopped into his chair and let his long athletic legs dangle over the arms. The movement drew Heralda's attention. He was everything in the world she shouldn't want. Copper hair, flawless skin that glowed, and eyes that twinkled so that he actually seemed to be a flaming light. What in the world would the mistress of dark magicks do with the master of arts and passions? Well, some ideas did come to her mind, but Culain had been far too busy bedding her creations the past six millennia to take notice of her. "What do you want to do about this, Culain?"

At length, he sighed, then looked around. "Did any of you interfere with my peeps?" Silence. "Did any of you do anything that would cause the royal

house of fae to mate the royal house of elves?"
Silence. "Very well then. 'Tis a trick of fate. Nothing more."

"Okaaay. Do you want Kellareal to help them or stay out of it?"

"Yeah." He looked at Heralda until she began to feel uncomfortable and squirm just a little. Then he grinned. Bastard. "What do you want?"

"I'm a woman, Culain. That means I vote for true love."

He cocked his head. "True love. The mating instinct isn't true love, love. It's mating instinct. Not the same thing at all."

"No?"

"No."

"Then what is true love?"

"Who says I believe in true love?"

It was Heralda's turn to stare. At length she said, "Yes. I think we should allow our Enforcer to help them." Her head jerked toward Hu as if she'd received a jolt of brilliance.

"What!"

"Hu."

"What!"

"We *do* need to find Etana."

"Why?"

"Because it's a perfect opportunity for a mediator. When Kellareal moves the young couple to a different ring, the ruling families, who will also be grieving families, may be of a mind to negotiate for a real and lasting peace." She turned toward Culain. "Assuming that's what you want."

Culain waved his hand in dismissal. In turn,

Heralda nodded at Hu, who, said, "Yep. Perfect. How do we find her?"

Once Ming was on a roll, he couldn't be derailed easily. "And what about Theasophie's religion gene? Now *there* was a great idea!"

Theasophie looked up from her tarot spread. "They needed an outlet for the spiritual side of their natures."

"That's what they've got us for."

"Oh. Us, is it? We're no better than they are," Heralda said.

"We don't have to be *better* to be worshipped. We used to have to do tricks from time to time. Now we don't have to do anything. Thanks to Theasophie's little experiment, if we weren't here, I think they'd make us up." Ming stood in front of the centerpiece in the room. It was a large holograph of the Earth spinning with its web of thousands of dimensions rising horizontally, circling, connected to the planet like an anchor. Each of the cells in the web was a reflection of that dimension that could be targeted or enlarged if any member of the Council wanted to see something specific.

"Right," said Rager. "I've always thought that blind worship was one of their better qualities."

Ignoring Rager, the others looked at each other. Culain spoke up. "Maybe, but I'm thinking Pierce and Prick Posse won't agree. Could be hard to cover without notice now."

"We would have caught it earlier if someone hadn't gotten lost in his little games when it was his watch." Ming was looking at Huber.

"Two words, Ming. Perfect storm," said Hu.

Ming sniffed and turned away. "Remember what happened when you tried to hide the fact that you gave crystal technology to Atlanteans by cleaning it up with water? It spawned myths all over about great floods, disappearing continents. Pierce went volcanic. He was literally foaming at the mouth. You remember that?" He looked around for confirmation.

"Look," said Heralda. "We agreed when we set all this in motion that we'd take turns watching the project. When everybody does their bit, it works. The trouble occurs when one of us comes up in the rotation and loses focus because he has the attention span of a human."

Everyone looked at Hu.

"That's right, Huber. I'm talking to you. Remember the Witch Trials in Volsrave Dimension? When Thee's children were torturing mine? You were off watching pirates in the Caribbean."

He looked anything but remorseful.

Heralda shook her head. "Okay, Theasophie needs to stop playing Solitaire sometime this century and deal with her religion gene mess before we have another Inquisition that no one is expecting."

"Ha! Oh!" Hu clapped. "Inquisition that no one is expecting. Heralda. You're my favorite."

She went on. "Right now let's see if we can score redemption points by solving this little problem with Culain's kids. What do they call themselves?" she asked Kellareal.

"Elves and fae."

"Elves and fae. They don't know they're the same." She glanced at Culain.

Heralda loved Culain's children like she loved

her own. Each one of them had something of him in them. If they couldn't sing, they could dance. If they couldn't dance, they could spin a tale. If they couldn't bind a spell with a story, they could light a room with the twinkle of an eye. If they couldn't be optimistic, they could joke about their misfortune. He was the very embodiment of the Earth plane.

"Now, these two pretty children are compelled to each other because of our mating impulse. Let's fix this."

Huber looked at Heralda closely. "Why is it so important to you, Magick?" She blushed. "You're a romantic!" Huber squeed and clapped his hands. "It has something to do with that vampire, doesn't it? Tell us. Tell us what it is."

"It has nothing, or, er, little to do with the vampire." She blushed harder and glanced toward Culain, but his attention was fully occupied with a Rubik's cube.

"What you're working on then? What is it?"

"What I've been working on? Um, well, I was thinking that it would be interesting to see what a fully actualized coupling looked like."

"Which language are you speaking right now?"

"Social science. I mean, males and females experience sexual completion in entirely different ways."

"From the standpoint of brain chemistry," Ming interjected.

"Hmmm. They're created in our image, but there's a flaw in the design. Regardless of rumors about 'coming hard'," she put that in air quotes, "males always have the exact same orgasm. On a scale of one to five, it's a five every time. Maybe they care who their partner is before and after, but during? No. Not at all.

"When you scan their brains during climax, there's a little portion that lights up. Look there. See that red spot. Females, on the other hand. Well, it's like the stuff they sell at the fireworks trailer. Look here at the range. Tiny pop to whole brain light up explosive. I thought it would be an improvement on design if males could experience what females experience and the only way I could think of to create a shared experience was to have them ingest the chemicals flowing through veins near the brain."

She flushed again when she realized that Culain had stopped what he was doing and was looking at her with genuine interest for the first time in, well, ever. "And what was your conclusion regarding that experiment?"

She smiled at Culain, loving that she had his interest for a moment. "Would you like to observe?"

Culain came close enough that she felt his breath on her face. "No. I don't want to observe." He bent to her ear. "I want to participate. Show me."

"Ahem."

"Oh. Kellareal. Sorry. Didn't mean to leave you waiting. Go grab the kids and find a suitable place to put them. Find Etana, fill her in on the details. Tell her we want her to come up with a story and sort this mess out." He bowed. "You can go."

"Thank you."

CHAPTER 11

Elora reached for the phone, hoping to stop the ringing before it woke Helm.

"Hello?" she whispered.

"You need to get up and get dressed. I'm coming to get you."

When she heard Litha's voice she came fully awake and sat on the side of the bed. "What? Why?"

"Just do it. I'll explain. I'll be in your living room in three minutes."

"What is it?" Ram sounded sleepy, but was alert.

"Litha will be in our living room in three, um, two and a half minutes. I'm supposed to be dressed. She'll explain."

"Okay." He found jeans where he'd left them on a chair and drug them up his body commando. He walked into the bath, swirled mouthwash, and ran a hand through his hair. A day's growth of beard didn't look bad on Ram because it was so blonde. He heard a rustle in the front part of the apartment. "She's here."

"I'm hurrying. I need another two minutes."

Ram found Litha in the kitchen. He walked straight to the coffee server and looked at her. "You want?"

She hesitated then said, "Yes. That would be

helpful."

"She says she needs two minutes."

"Okay."

"This about my sister?"

"Yes."

"'Tis good?"

He looked and sounded so hopeful, she was glad to get to be the one to tell him it was going to work out. "Yeah."

Ram smiled and nodded. "I'm no' mad about the London shoppin' trip. I know you have plausible deniability."

"I don't know what you mean."

He found that snicker-worthy, even if it was too early to be funny.

"If he's laughing, it must be good news." Elora came in, still straightening a sweater. "Got some of that for me?"

"Comin' up." He looked at Litha. "Tell."

Litha turned to Ram. "Maybe you should leave first. I'm offering you plausible deniability."

He laughed. "Whether I deny or no' 'twill be determined, but no one is expecting plausibility from me. Consider me cautioned and proceed."

"Okay. I have this friend who's an elemental, calls himself an angel, but… you know."

Ram and Elora looked at each other as if to silently say, "No. We don't know."

"He works for this group called The Council. I don't know what they are exactly, but they're a species that's way, way, way out of our league. Anyway, they maintain a kind of handbook for behavior of species that can travel interdimensionally, like myself. In other words, I couldn't just pick you up and drop you in another dimension without the kind of trouble nobody ever wants to be in.

"So my friend suggested that we grant Aelsong and her mate sanctuary somewhere off world until we can get some peace negotiated between the elves and fae, but we had to get permission first."

"So you got permission?" asked Elora.

"Yes. Better than that. We got permission and they're going to send someone to mediate between your family," she looked at Ram, "and the fae."

"Litha. You did it." Elora was looking and sounding a little awestruck.

Litha laughed. "Well, yeah. Isn't that what you were expecting? You *did* call me."

Elora rushed her and gave her a big hug. "You're the best."

"That's right. You're still embarrassing me."

"So why am I getting dressed in the middle of the night?"

"You're going to be the cushion." Ram was leaning against the kitchen counter with his arms crossed and his lips pinched between two fingers. He and Elora exchanged a look. "I started thinking about how alarming it would be for the prince to have anyone simply appear in his secure quarters, much less a stranger asking to lay hands on his person so that he can spirit him away to another world."

"I see what you mean." Elora's gaze flicked to Ram and back to Litha. "So you think that if I, being someone he knows and trusts, appear in his quarters, he'll be more inclined to go peaceably."

"That's what I was thinking. So my plan is to

go get Aelsong. My friend is going to take you to talk to the prince and then bring him to an undisclosed location that neither of you would be able to divulge upon questioning by Ram's family."

"And Elora is bein' left behind?" Ram asked. "I assume that someone will be gettin' my mate out of the prince's apartment before someone discovers that he is no' there and she is?"

"There is that risk, but it's pretty small, a two or three minute window. I'm going to drop Song and go right back for Elora."

"That's no problem," Elora said. "It's pretty unlikely, but if someone does catch me there with the prince inexplicably missing, I'll just say he stepped out for a moment. By the time they're able to process and form words, you'll be there."

"And you think it would no' be a problem to say that no' only is the prince missin', but two women were first there and then no'?"

"Nobody believes stuff like that, Ram."

He lifted both his eyebrows and shoulders, then dropped both abruptly. "Okay, then. Have fun."

Elora stepped over and gave Ram a kiss on the ear, which never failed to make him smile. "Message for your sister?"

"Oh, aye. Tell her all will be well."

"I will."

He caught her back as she turned away and spoke low into her ear. "You're *my* cushion. Be safe."

Third Floor, North Wing, Holyrood Palace,

Edinburgh

Elora and Litha emerged from the passes and came to such an abrupt stop that it made Elora both dizzy and queasy. Apparently Litha felt like there wasn't much room for error and, of course, she'd been right. The shadowed close had extremely narrow walls, but a good view of both the palace and pedestrian traffic a few steps away on High Street.

"Elora Laiken, this is my friend, Kellareal."

Elora took his hand and tried not to stare, but it wasn't easy. The combination of white blonde hair and black eyes was so exotic it was disconcerting. It took her a minute to realize that those eyes reminded her of Deliverance.

"Hello. Wow." She looked at Litha. "He's even taller than Kay."

Litha chuckled. "He is. So we all know what we're doing?"

They nodded.

"Let me check it out and make sure he's alone," Kellareal said. Elora opened her mouth to say, "Okay," but closed it when she realized she would have been responding to air.

She turned to Litha, wrapped her arms around her middle and jumped up and down in place. "You know some of us are at the mercy of weather."

"Oh, sorry, I didn't think…" Litha's gaze jerked back to Elora. "I could start a fire."

Elora laughed loudly enough to make one person on High Street turn their head to see who was in the little alley. Luckily, they turned the other way before Kellareal reappeared.

"He's alone. Looks like a good time." The angel looked at Litha with enough affection to imitate a crush. "I'll take him and then come back for her. Get her ready."

Litha nodded. "Thank you."

He just smiled and wrapped his huge hand around Elora's forearm.

"Whoa. Whoa. Whoa. Wait a second. Where are the cuffs?"

"Cuffs?"

"You have something to tie us together to make sure I don't get lost?"

Kellareal smiled at Elora indulgently and nodded in understanding. "The demon. I'm not Deliverance. But I don't want you to stress, so…" He swooped her up like she weighed nothing and she clung to his neck reflexively, but before she had a chance to process any of that, they were standing in Duff's bedroom.

He was on the bed, lying on his side, looking out the high leaded glass windows.

They had left him a TV, since it couldn't be used for communication, and he'd used it to see pictures of Song. Since the story broke, the entertainment news had been full of stories about the two of them. They had even hastily pieced together documentaries about their childhoods. When Duff could find something with pictures of Aelsong, he watched. Otherwise, he wasn't interested.

Elora and the angel stood at the foot of the bed.

"Duff."

She said his name quietly, but his body still

jerked. He sat up. He recognized Elora instantly, but that alone couldn't explain away the alarm of having people poof into his father's version of a gilded cage.

"Duff, I know this is hard to process, but try to be calm while I explain. You have friends who are trying to help you. This is one of them. His name is Kellareal and he's an angel." Duff looked at the angel, but scowled in disbelief. "You know The Order deals with subjects that are too sensitive for general knowledge." She pointed at the angel. "Well, he comes within the scope of their activities. We're going to take you to Song."

At that Duff stood up. Even in the darkened room, Elora could see that he looked awful. "Song?"

"Yes. Litha is with her right now getting her ready to meet you. Do you know who Litha is?" He shook his head. "She's a very close friend of mine and Rammel's and Song knows her. I came so that you wouldn't be afraid to go with Kellareal. He can only take one of us. He's going to leave me here and come back for me after you and Song are situated."

Duff started to ask a question, but his voice sounded rough. He cleared his throat. "Situated where?"

She smiled. "All I know is that it will be safe, you'll be with your mate, and you'll have a lot more freedom that you do at this moment."

Duff stared at her for a second longer, then looked at the angel. "Let's go."

After a few minutes Kellareal set Duff down in a large empty dome-shaped room with mezzanine galleries encircling the perimeter all the way to the top. The walls were made from something that resembled smooth, seamless, ivory porcelain. Transparencies of live imagery moved over the walls which gave the vast room a feeling of being alive. There were scenes that were familiar as well as some that were exotic and terribly strange.

"What is this place?" Duff asked.

"It's the vestibule of the Council's chambers. Those are the people I work for. If you will wait here for a few minutes, I will return with your mate." Duff nodded and looked around, noting that there was no furniture. "Do you need to sit while you wait?"

"No. No' at all. Or, if I do, I'm no' opposed to sittin' on the floor." He looked down. "It looks very clean."

The angel smiled. "Well, your Highness, I hope she wants you as much as I'm told, because 'clean' is more than I can say for you." And he was gone.

It was true that Duff had paid no attention to grooming since his return. He ran his hand over his face feeling the scratch of beard and looked down at his rumpled clothing. Taking stock, he didn't know where he was except that he was alone in a room that could have been the set of a science fiction movie. His feelings bounced back and forth between excitement about the possibility of seeing Aelsong, which he wouldn't entirely believe until it happened, anxiety over the unknown, and the self-consciousness that the angel had planted just before he left.

Altogether, the cocktail of emotion made sitting out of the question even though he was definitely weak from not eating.

There was no sound whatever in the dome vestibule where he paced, but there was an echo with such enormous amplification that each of his breaths sounded like wind rushing. At one point he thought he could hear his own heartbeat. The shush of air and tiny pop that would be inaudible in his normal reality was loud enough to make him turn toward the sound, just in time to open his arms before Aelsong rushed into him.

He crushed her body to him and felt every tremor she was feeling. She wasn't crying so that her vocal chords were engaged, but her body was quaking and her breathing was ragged. He closed his eyes and held on for dear life, putting his cheek against her wet hair. *Wet hair?*

"Your hair is wet," he said softly.

"Yes," said the angel. "Women think reuniting with the love of their lives justifies taking a minute for a shower. Wait here. I'll be back in a minute."

They heard people talking momentarily, like someone had opened a door and then closed it, but they didn't let go of each other or look up.

"Are you well then?" Duff said close to her ear.

The tremors in her body were beginning to subside, but she was clinging to him like he was the branch that was her lifeline above a thousand foot drop.

"Maybe now," she said so quietly it was almost a whisper.

"Here," he said, trying to pull back just a little, "let me have a look at you."

She angled her head back so that he could look into her face. At the same time, she got a look at him. "Do you think they'll be havin' razors where we're goin'?"

He smiled. "Judgin' from our rescuer's comments, I'd imagine so. You feel so good to me. I guess I'm needin' somethin' only you can give."

"'Twas horrible, Duffy."

The door opened and Kellareal walked toward them accompanied by a little man with a contagious smile. He had a little pot belly which seemed to be accentuated by the fact that he was wearing a white toga, black combat boots, and a laurel wreath on his head. When they came close, they could see that his eyes were an unusual amber color and the irises appeared to have concentric circles that moved in waves. They were compelling in the sense that it was impossible not to lean forward and investigate to confirm whether or not it was a trick of the light.

"Duff Torquil, Aelsong Hawking, this is Huber Quizno. He's one of your hosts who has granted you sanctuary until this can be worked out satisfactorily between your families and their respective peoples."

"How do you do?" said the prince. "And thank you for your hospitality. My mate and I are grateful." He glanced at Aelsong. "Very grateful. Might I ask where we are?"

Hu nodded. "No. Sorry. If it makes you feel any better though, it wouldn't do a thing for you if I told you. Come with me. I'll show you to your room."

He appeared to be walking into a wall. Duff guided Song forward and continued to follow, but looked back at Kellareal to be sure he was bringing up the rear. The prince had no idea what they were walking into and he didn't like the virtual blindfold. The only reason he had to trust that any of the strange events were in their best interest was that Elora seemed to have faith in the plan. Not much to go on, but at least he had a firm grip on his mate, more than he could say he had expected an hour before. And he knew she was real. That just couldn't be faked.

Whatever it was that was coming next, they would be together.

When they neared the wall, it opened up into a wide hallway decorated in the same style as the vestibule. They walked past four doors then stopped in front of the fifth door on the right. "Here you are," said Hu, motioning them to enter.

They stepped onto a grass path in front of a thatch roof cottage, next to a stream, with blooming flowers that would put most botanical gardens to shame.

"Duffy." Song's voice was full of wonder.

"Aye, love?"

"This place… This is the cottage from my favorite story my grandmother used to read to me."

Duff looked from her to the little house and cocked his head. "You like it then."

She put her arms around his neck. "I more than like it. It's a dream come true."

"Right then," said Hu. "If you decide to seek out company, just follow that path. It will take you to the village. You're completely safe. The weather is perfect. Always. There are no political boundaries. It's true sanctuary to everyone here, including yourselves. When we have word that it's safe for you to return to your reality, we'll send the Enforcer."

"Enforcer?" Duff balked at the sound of that.

Hu waved his hand at Kellareal. "Sorry. I mean the angel. Him. Anyhooooo, meanwhile, have fun. Don't do anything I wouldn't do." He started away.

Kellareal leaned over Duff's shoulder. "Razors are inside." He handed Duff a cell phone that was super thin and had no brand. "If you need anything, you can send me a text on this."

"Hold on. I, sorry, I truly do no' want to sound ungrateful, but what shall we do about basics such as, em, food?"

"This place is what you would probably call, um, magical? Consider this a respite from challenge. If you want food, just go to the kitchen and say what you want. Think of this as your honeymoon." He looked at the cottage recreated from Song's special memory. "Honeymoon cottage. Enjoy yourselves."

Song and Duff stood in front of the picturesque little storybook house. He reached down and opened the waist-high gate and bowed to indicate she should go through first. When they reached the porch, he stopped her.

"Let me go first." He opened the door, but saw nothing except a cheerful interior. He poked his head into the kitchen and bedroom. "Come then. Looks to be as they said."

They explored the cottage together. Each of them came across multiple objects, scattered around the house, that were exact replicas of sentimental objects, right down to a nick or chip or tear. There were two doors that appeared to be shallow cupboards, but when opened, were large walk-in closets stocked with their favorite mild weather clothes.

Both wanted to do as their guide recommended and simply enjoy, but each new discovery increased their feelings of uneasiness. The forced separation was as traumatic physically for a mated pair as emotionally. They'd been betrayed by a prominent head of government who had promised them political asylum. They'd been torn from each other by force and then imprisoned by their own families. Neither was feeling particularly trusting at the moment, Duff all the more because he wasn't privy to the unusual aspects of Aelsong's personal and professional reality.

Unfortunately, their rescuers had failed to take that into account.

Duff sat down on a cheery floral-covered window seat and texted Kellareal.

Duff: *Can I talk to Elora?*

Ten minutes later a chime, that didn't originate in the phone, sounded to let him know there was a reply. Kellareal: *Is there something you need?*

Duff: *Yes. We need to know whether or not we can trust this. I want to talk to my sister-in-law.*

When no response was received, Duff sighed and looked at his mate, who was watching him with a worried look, which he hated seeing on her beautiful face. He managed a little smile.

"Did I mention how much I missed you?" The tension in her brow cleared. She returned his smile and shook her head. He reached up and ran a hand over the scratch of his beard. "Give me ten minutes to clean up a bit?" She nodded.

While Song waited, she walked around and looked out the windows. They were open. No screens. No need. She could hear both birdsong and the gurgling sound of the little stream where a tiny waterfall broke near the cottage.

"Are you hungry? You look like you have no' eaten for a while."

"You sayin' I'm too skinny for ye?" Duff looked blank. "Just kiddin'. Do no' look so worried. I will no' bite unless you ask me to." She let her eyes drift down his frame. He looked good cleaned up, but definitely tired and definitely thinner. "When was the last time you had a repast worth notin'?"

"Same as you." He smiled. "But my appetite could be returnin'."

He held out his hand indicating that they would go to the kitchen and try out food summoning magic together. They stood in the tiny kitchen for some time. There were no appliances of any kind, just counter, sink, cutting board and cabinets with painted pottery that added to the feeling of warmth.

He raised her hand that he was holding to his lips and brushed his lips over her knuckles. "How do you think this works?"

"Great Paddy. 'Tis a riddle. Should we just decide on a dish and say it aloud? Maybe?"

He stared into Song's eyes as he said, "Beef Wellington." Looking at each other they both saw something in peripheral vision, but they didn't look away. They just started to laugh. Duff said, "One. Two. Three."

On three they both turned toward the counter and indeed, a fine Beef Wellington sizzled on a bronzed platter surrounded by roast potatoes, sautéed asparagus, and steamed carrots. For convenience sake, a knife and meat fork were set next to the dish in invitation. It was an invitation that Duff accepted promptly. He sliced into the middle of the rolled cut, pulled it apart, and looked up at Song. "Just the way I like it."

He cut off a one inch sliver and used his fingers to put it in his mouth. "Hmmm," he said as he followed that with a small roasted new potato, then a spear of asparagus and a carrot. He was making yummy sounds of male satisfaction that only eating good food with fingers while standing in the kitchen can inspire. And it was making Song's mouth water.

Duff held up a piece of meat, but Song shook her head as she said, "Lobster Thermidor."

Without delay, a mouth-watering version of Lobster Thermidor appeared on a bed of green beans almondine. She shook her head and said, "No. Green peas on the side with…," she glanced at Duff with mischief in her eye, "macaroni and cheese." The plate disappeared and reappeared as ordered. "The steam risin' is an extra nice touch, is it no'?"

She laughed, but wasted no time tearing a bit of lobster off with her own fingers. Of course they could have seated themselves at the little table with the charming distressed finish, but it had been a while since they'd wanted to eat and the return of appetite was joyful. They were happy to simply stand at the counter, eat with fingers, feed each other and giggle. The nearness of each other and the weight of food in stomachs had given them both such a feeling of well-being, that their apprehensions had begun to recede.

The phone rang. Or at least there was a ring that came from somewhere.

Duff looked at the plain black device. He could see Elora on the face. "Hello? Duff?"

"Elora. Can you see me?"

"No. Your image is blocked. Can you see me?"

"Aye. I see you."

"Can you put the phone on speaker so both of you can hear me or see me or whatever?"

"Aye."

"Okay. I understand you asked to talk to me?"

"We do no' mean to be a bother, but there are many thin's about this situation that are no' explicable."

"I'll level with you. I'm not privy to every detail myself, but I will reassure you as much as I can. I wouldn't put Song in a situation that was questionable. There is nothing that I wouldn't trust Litha with. There's nothing I haven't trusted her with. And, if she trusts Kellareal, then you're as safe as safe can be.

"Song, I think, under the circumstances, you should compromise your vow to The Order – to the extent that you are now affected, and tell Duff what you know about Litha and about how our world is comprised of a lot of different realities, one of which you're questioning right now."

"Oh, aye, I do think that would be helpful," Song replied. "Will we be talkin' to you again, do you think?"

"Probably not until this is over. Ram is on his way to see your family right now. They've discovered that you're not there and they've received word that you've been granted sanctuary by a benefactor who chooses to remain anonymous so that there is no chance that your location may be leaked. Of course, they wonder about the escape, but that will just have to be an unsolved mystery. Like that train heist."

Elora thought she heard a sniffle. "Ram's goin' to help us?"

"Yes, Song. And, you were right about him not staying mad if I told him why I did it."

"You sound surprised."

"I do not."

"Just kiddin'. Thank you. Again. And tell him I love him."

The three said goodbye. Duff set the device down on the table. "So what is it she's thinkin' you'll be tellin' me?"

The Scotia monarchy were aware of The Order's activities up to a point. It was necessary partly because of the location of headquarters in Edinburgh and partly because Edinburgh was a city that had been plagued by vampire since before the plagues. The scope of activities reached further than their fae hosts could have guessed and that scope seemed to be growing exponentially.

Song glanced at Duff then said, "White wine," to the ceiling.

Duff's gaze followed Song as she picked up the gold liquid and drank deep. "Will I be needin' scotch whiskey?"

CHAPTER 12

Tepring Hawking had lingered in her quarters extra long, but she was old enough to know that staying in bed wasn't going to solve anything. Her face was so swollen from crying that she had cancelled her appointments indefinitely. She sat at her desk in a belted silk dress and stared out the window at the sheep grazing on the terraced meadows just beyond the gardens. There was a quiet knock at the door.

She supposed it was Rammel and she hoped it was. He was due to arrive early afternoon. She couldn't think of a single other person she would rather see, except for Song, of course.

Thinking that caused the tears to start all over. She reached up to staunch the flow, but to her great consternation, her emotions were in control. That was unacceptable. A person who had served for decades as mistress of the palace, first as the king's wife and then as the king's mother, should be able to manage a modicum of control over her own bodily functions.

"Aye. Come in then."

"Madam, a phone call for you."

"I told you no calls today."

"This one says she will no' take no for an answer."

"Well, for Paddy's sake, Loftis. Who is it then?"

"Lorna Torquil, ma'am."

Tepring froze. "Put her through."

The queen's secretary withdrew and closed the door. Tepring listened for the catch. The old doors were solid and well-built. If the latch caught properly, she could be reasonably assured of privacy for a conversation, barring spy equipment. For office use, she was still using an old-fashioned multiline, land phone. Aelsblood insisted the wireless technology not be used for official communications because he didn't believe it was secure enough.

"Your Highness."

"Your Grace."

"Is she well?"

There was a slight pause before the Scotia queen answered. "Aelsong? Do you no' know?"

"Is she with you?"

"No. I was callin' for your reassurance that my son is well. He disappeared and then we received a message that the two of them have been given sanctuary and that we will no' be seein' him again unless we reach an accord with elves that includes open sanction of the marriage."

Tepring sighed. "Aye, sounds exactly like the missive that was delivered to my son, the king. He was certain it was some fae trickery."

"Aye. My husband thought the same only the phrase was Irish hijinks. May I ask you, if you hear anythin' more, will you be callin'? I give you my promise it will go no further. 'Tis for my peace of mind alone."

"'Tis your only child, aye?"

"He is. And she's your only girl."

"An agreement then? Whatever is learned is

shared?"

"Done."

Both of the royal households were thrown into a state of turmoil when they received a letter stating that they would not see their children again unless they managed to secure the peace for both peoples for now and the future. Initially both kings rejected the leveraged suggestion that talks should commence.

However, after considerable grousing and grumbling, ranting and raving, the fae king had agreed to a meeting. That was in large part due to the efforts of the fae queen, who had used every manner of pressure available to her to persuade him to make peace with the elves, including threats of suicide, and in smaller part due to the ruler's feelings about his son personally and about what it would mean to leave Scotia without an heir.

A peace talks meeting was arranged at a neutral site in London by the anonymous party and a mediator was appointed - a supposedly well-respected woman named Arles Logature, who was Etana disguised as human.

Every staff member who was in the east part of the palace at Derry heard Ram come through the side door by the topiaries and shout, "Honey! I'm home!" And each one who had been employed by the household when Ram was a sometimes resident turned to another and smiled, thinking he would be a welcome relief to the pall that had fallen not only over the household, but to some extent, over the entire country.

Ethelred's two Irish wolfhounds, whose hearing could detect sounds originating in the palace from great distance, attempted to knock over two people and one statue on their wild and heedless mission to capture a greeting. He had made it as far as the grand central staircase when the dogs caught up to him. He had never so much appreciated Elora's insistence that big dogs need to be taught good manners than when the two giant hounds knocked him off his feet. They licked and sniffed wherever Black had touched and wiggled their enormous bodies like they were puppies.

Just as Ram was getting them calmed down he heard footsteps on the marble tile.

"You should no' play with the dogs on the floor, Rammel. 'Tis a bad habit."

"Aye, Da. 'Tis good to see you as well. And where would the queen mum be keepin' herself on this fine chill overcast and thoroughly Irish day?"

Ethelred looked toward the staircase. "She's been stayin' close to her rooms. Does no' like to be seen lookin' red and puffy. Still vain, you know?"

"Should I take some tea?"

Ram's father shook his head. "No. She'd rather be seein' you sooner than later."

Rammel began to climb the stairs, but looked back as he did. His father's semi-cordial tone was a little discomfiting. People grow into a rhythm of expectation, particularly in the area of family relations. Having someone step out of their role disrupts that rhythm and creates confusion.

Tepring had not moved from her chair after her conversation with the fae queen. There was a soft knock on the door.

"What is it now, Loftis?"

"'Tis no' Loftis. 'Tis Ram."

She swung around in her chair, took one look at him, and burst into a fresh session of tears. After getting a big hug, Ram rekindled the fire and gently coaxed his mum to sit in one of the two overstuffed chairs in front of the fire.

"I'm askin' for tea, Mum. Is there somethin' in particular you'd like or will you have your usual?"

"Whiskey and arsenic."

"Mum," Ram chuckled. "You should no' even joke about such thin's."

"Who's jokin'?"

Ram opened the door and stuck his head out. "We could use a tray. Bewley's Irish Afternoon and gingerbread scones. Ask them to bring us some honey butter and maple butter." Pause. "No. I do no' want milk and I do no' want half milk. I want cream, real cream. As a matter of fact, I want heavy cream. Do no' laugh. I'm bein' serious."

He closed the door and sat down next to his mother.

"Now then, Mum. Are you familiar with the phrase drama queen?"

She saw his mouth twitch. "'Tis nothin' funny about this, Rammel. I can no' lose one of my children. As if I have one to spare."

"No one is suggestin' so. Only sayin' that we do no' cry wolf unless there really is one."

"What are you talking about?"

Ram realized that he'd spent so much time with Elora he sometimes forgot that some of her expressions were unfamiliar to others. "Oh. 'Tis just a reference to a silly story. Ne'er mind at all."

She sniffed. "You look good, Rammel. Have you seen your father?"

"On the way up."

"Ah. How did he seem?"

Ram pursed his lips and looked at the fire like he was trying to decide how to answer. "Mellow. Subdued."

She nodded. "Your brother left for London. 'Twas difficult enough to e'en get him to go. I do no' know what is the bother with him."

"Has that somethin' to do with Song?"

"Aye. Everythin'."

She told him about the first message concerning the threat that they would not see their children again if they did not make peace and bless the mating. And about the second message outlining details for a forced negotiation. There was a postscript to the second message urging them to watch a special documentary broadcast to be aired on the History Channel that night. It claimed that important information pertinent to the discussion at hand would be presented.

Rammel had dinner with his parents. He couldn't remember having ever had dinner, just the three of them, in his life. There was a tiny dining room decorated in the dark wood style of an eighteenth century tavern. The three of them ate together in front of the fire.

Ram was curious to know about the general reaction to the elopement. He was told that there were factions calling for the Hawkings to surrender the monarchy. The hardest thing for his parents was hearing descriptions of Song. The most polite words were often disgrace and traitor. Ram felt a shameful blush creeping up his neck when he recalled that his first reaction had been to use that same word.

Ethelred looked at his watch. "'Tis time for the tele presentation if you're still wantin' to view it."

They adjourned to a small parlor that was outfitted in the modern style of comfortable furniture. A Welsh professor had been given information about the political histories of elves and fae by an Irishman. The professor had gone to the sites mentioned in the evidence he'd been given and found sufficient reason to believe the claims of the tale that elves and fae were the same people when they had first arrived in the Brit Isles and that the root of the millennia-long war was a family feud over a mating.

Ram took this revelation in stride since he'd already heard the story, but he could tell that his parents were stunned. When it was over, Ethelred said nothing, but walked to the liquor cache and poured himself a scotch. As an afterthought, as if he'd just remembered he wasn't alone, he turned and lifting the glass said, "Anyone else?"

Ram said, "Still on American time. 'Tis early for me."

Tepring said, "Give me a double." She looked at Ram. "Do you think any of it could be true?"

"Aye. I work with an elf who needed an emergency blood transfusion last year. There was no' elf blood available, but there was fae blood. When I protested, they laughed and said 'twas the same."

"I had always wondered…" Ethelred began, but didn't finish the sentence. "I wonder what Blood will do, or not do, with this information."

"What will you do with it, Da?" Ram asked.

Ethelred gave his son a thorough appraisal, then said, "The next time I encounter fae, I will probably hesitate before I begin throwin' rocks."

Ram laughed. Tepring rolled her eyes.

Etana was an introvert at her core, but she had been given a talent for guiding others through negotiations to resolve disputes and hoped that the children of Danu weren't as intractable as others said.

"No one ever wants to compromise, your Highness. But the alternative would be to carry a twin blade ax and lop off the head of everyone who disagrees with you until the day you encounter someone with a different perspective and a faster, sharper ax."

"Do no' patronize me, young lady. Who are you again and what is your interest in this matter? If you be neither elf nor fae, I fail to grasp that you have a say." Ritavish Torquil, the fae king, was visibly irritated and wishing that Ethelred was still king of Ireland. There was an elf he could at least respect, one with whom civil conversation was possible.

That traditional regard between leaders was what had enabled the elves and fae to be at war in name only for the past several centuries. They held each other at bay with mutual distaste, but without actual bloodshed. The fae king knew that any reasonable head of state would naturally see the wisdom in maintaining the status quo. Since sitting down for talks with the young elf king, he was having misgivings about whether or not the boy understood that.

"I don't have a say in the outcome, although that would certainly simplify and expedite. What I do have a say in is how the proceedings proceed. So, once again, can we agree on the starting point that both parties will have to find flexibility in order for us to reach accord."

"O' course," said Ritavish.

"So far, Ms. Logature, I've heard nothin' to indicate an understandin' of the crux of the matter."

"What is your view of the crux of the matter, Your Highness?"

"Motivation."

Etana, in the guise of Arles Logature, showed no emotion. "Would you care to expand that thought?"

"Certainly. You're after compromise. You can pretty it up with words like flexibility all you want and it still comes down to one thin', givin' in. I'm no' sayin' there's ne'er a reason to do so, but I am sayin' that one of us is powerfully motivated, while the other is no'."

Reading between the lines of what Aelsblood was saying, Etana allowed the smallest flicker of a scowl to read on her features, thereby betraying her distaste for the elf and his comments.

The meeting quickly degenerated into a

standing yell rather than a seated talk. It became clear to Etana that Aelsblood had only agreed to the meeting for the opportunity to grandstand to his people and not because of a sincere approach to the subject with mind and heart open to change.

By midafternoon the television channels were playing Aelsblood's parting comments so often the sound bite was almost on loop. Ram stood in his father's study readying to watch the replay. His mother sat stiffly, spine straight, with a handkerchief in her hand. The necessity of his mother needing a handkerchief close by at all times made Ram frown.

When Aelsblood emerged from the stately old Greco-Roman building that housed the Foreign and Commonwealth Office, he was surrounded by security holding back a throng of reporters. Though he may have appeared to be grim to those who didn't know him, his family recognized the look in his eye and set of his mouth as enjoying the attention. For the moment, he was not the ruler of a small country that was insignificant on the world stage. He was the focal point of all eyes around the world and he clearly planned to make the most of it.

He paused on the steps.

"Your Highness, are you leaving the peace talks without resolution?"

"If the fae prince is no' returned, the fae are left with no heir apparent. Therefore, they have more to lose in the bargain than elves. When they begin to exhibit a proper appreciation of that, there may be room for negotiation, but understand this, Ireland has no need to negotiate peace because my country is no' eager for the return of a traitor. They can keep my sister and good luck getting' their countrymen to accept an elf as queen."

Two dozen voices barked follow-up questions. He nodded at one. "What did you think of the presentation on the history of the conflict?"

The king made a dismissive noise. "Hogwash."

The camera followed until his limousine pulled away from the curb.

CHAPTER 13

With his arms crossed over his chest, Ram had watched Blood publicly throw their sister away. His mother had left the room sobbing. His father had switched off the tele with a remote, poured a whiskey and sat down heavily in his favorite chair. His dogs were lying on their sides between Ethelred's chair and the fire.

There was no sound in the room other than everyday sounds that serve as the score to contentment, or melancholy, or despair, all relative to the emotions of the perceiver. The faint patter of rain, a small crackle of fire, and an occasional sigh coming from one of the dogs.

As Ram had replayed the broadcast in his mind, over and over, he had felt his fingers curl into fists and was seeing flashes of red battle haze. At length he interrupted the everyday sounds that could serve as the score for contentment or melancholy, depending on one's viewpoint.

If he had been someone else, he might have seen Ethelred's study as a supremely comfortable masculine retreat with muted colors and furniture worn in such a way as to impart that the occupants lived in harmony with a long history. Since he wasn't someone else, he associated the room with memories of his father's disapproval, which was swiftly and invariably followed by whatever punishment his father thought appropriate.

He wished he could tell his father about his accomplishments. He wished he might have experienced the approval that Aelsblood took for granted. Just once. Maybe.

When Rammel broke the silence, it was to say, "I would very much like to kill my brother right now."

Ethelred looked up and met Ram's gaze. "Me, too."

Ram sat down in the chair across from his father. "I've always wondered, Da, why you passed the crown on to Blood? You were still young. A good king. Will you tell me?"

With a sigh he said, "I had observed that some monarchs with capable offsprin', held onto the throne 'til the end of their days, for so long that by the time they passed, the heir's time was passed as well. Did no' seem right to me. No' right or wise. So I thought to avoid the error and the regret."

"And did you avoid regret?"

Ethelred laughed softly and looked at Ram with sad eyes. "Am no' thinkin' so today. I would no' give a ha'penny for a man who would abandon a member of his family."

Ram saw a barrage of images of his childhood. He held no illusion that he hadn't been a difficult kid. He'd been practically impossible as a matter of fact. When he would run away to the New Forest and live alone like a feral child, his father hadn't abandoned him. He'd seen to it that Liam O'Torvall and the people of Black-on-Tarry had adopted him and were looking out for him like a community project. Whenever he came back home, he was welcomed. Whenever he couldn't stand to be there, he left and his father let him. If he looked at it honestly, through the eyes of an adult, he could see that it wasn't just to be rid of a troublemaker, that his father had done the best thing for him.

Ram sighed. "So what are you thinkin' we might do?"

"Do? I wish I knew. I'm receptive to suggestions if you have some."

"I might."

"Let's hear it. "

"I'm no' a constitutional scholar…." Ethelred snorted into his whiskey tumbler. "But if I remember correctly, the crown is yours for life unless you decide to give it up."

"Aye. 'Tis true."

"So I'm thinkin', if 'twas yours to give up, can you no' simply take it back?"

Ethelred barked out a short laugh, then looking closer at Ram, let his smile fade. "You're serious?"

"Aye."

"What makes you think that I would have it back in a hundred years?"

"Aelsong."

Ethelred stared at Ram for a full minute, then rose and walked to his desk that sat in the crescent of a large bay window at the end of the room. He picked up the phone. "I need to see Hogmanay Kilter. Find him and bring him to the palace right away."

"Who's that?" asked Ram.

"Someone who *is* a constitutional scholar."

"You're thinkin' about it."

Ethelred gave his son a look that could have been interpreted as a conspiratorial smile. "Thinkin' about somethin'." The phone rang. "Aye." Pause. "Very well. Show him to my study when he arrives." He replaced the receiver on the desk unit. "On his way. Should be just ten minutes or so."

Ram and his da passed the time by talking about Aelsblood's strengths and weaknesses as king. "Does he no' ask you for advice then, Da?"

"Ne'er."

"His loss."

Ethelred's eyes sparked a little at that and the corners of his mouth softened.

"Mr. Kilter, I do no' believe you've met my other son, Rammel."

The dogs lifted their heads to see if they approved of the new arrival, but seeing who it was, did not get up. Rather, they seemed mildly put out to have been disturbed from their nap.

"I've no' had the pleasure, your Highness." He nodded at Ram.

"Please," said Ethelred as he motioned to a chair, "sit down. What can we offer you? Tea? Coffee? Scotch?"

Kilter chuckled at the last offer. "If I return to the state's offices with scotch on my breath, my days in your employ might prove numbered, e'en if I protest that I could no' say no to the former king."

Ethelred laughed. "In that case, I withdraw the offer. Tea?"

"Coffee. With a teensy bit of Baileys perhaps. If you do no' mind."

That raised both of Ethelred's brows. He glanced at Ram, who was clearly enjoying the exchange. His da asked for Kilter's refreshment and then sat.

"This is a matter of strict confidentiality, Mr. Kilter. May we count on you to keep your cards close to your vest?"

"Certainly, Your...em, sir."

"I have a question about succession. When I gave up the throne, 'twas mine to give, as rights to the office expire with me. Is that correct so far?"

"One hundred percent, sir."

"Then here is my question for you, as authority on the subject. Does the office remain mine to give or *take* so long as I live?"

Kilter's eyes immediately began to twinkle. "I see what you are askin'. There's very little historical precedent, since so few monarchs have e'er passed the kingship willin'ly."

Ram answered the knock at the door. Mr. Kilter's tall steamy mug was set before him with a white linen napkin. The three men were silent until they were alone again.

Kilter took a sip. "'Tis excellent, sir. Thank you."

"You're welcome. You were sayin'..."

"Aye. There are few incidents of the throne bein' passed durin' the lifetime of the former ruler and, there has ne'er been a case of takin' it back. Although," he glanced between Ram and his father, "if you do no' mind me sayin' so, if e'er there was a case when such a thin' was deserved, this situation would get my vote.

"As you know, I'm more than familiar with the law regardin' succession. I can see no impediment to changin' your mind, should you wish to take back the throne. Nor is there any legal grounds on which the current king might mount formal protest."

"Aye. And what about takin' it back to give it to someone else?"

Ram's head jerked toward his father as his mind immediately started cataloging who in Paddy's name the man might have in mind for the job and what it would mean for his family to turn over the monarchy.

Kilter first looked surprised, then pursed his lips. The look of delight was replaced with one resembling worry. "I see no legal impediment barring that either."

Ethelred stood giving the distinct impression that the meeting was over. "Thank you, Kilter. You've been most helpful. Please take the coffee with you and do no' forget the confidence. Should it be violated, I might have to go medieval after I retake the throne and spike your head to the front gate."

"Aye, sir. Quite, sir," Kilter said as the door closed behind him.

Ethelred turned back to Rammel. "Sit down." The command and the air of authority brought a deluge of memories back for Ram. He took the chair across from his father. That encounter between the two of them was far different than the routine disciplining of a problem child.

Ethelred smiled at Ram openly. "How would

you like to be king?"

Ram shot out of his chair like it was on fire. "Me?"

"Sit down, son," Ethelred said quietly.

Ram hesitated like he was deciding whether to acquiesce to his father's request to be seated or bolt for the door. He sat. Then laughed.

"Good one, Da. For just a second there, I thought you might be serious," Ram said, shaking his head.

Ethelred laughed with him. "E'en if you're thinkin' 'tis a very fine joke, I am serious nonetheless."

Ram shook his head. "You're no'."

Ethelred nodded. "I am."

"Da. That makes no sense. I'm the family fuck up, remember? I'm the *last* person who should be king. You must be feelin' truly desperate to come up with such a half-assed idea. You do no' e'en like me. Remember?"

Ethelred's smile vanished and was replaced by a look of genuine surprise. "Do no' like you? Whate'er gave you such a thought, Rammel?"

Ram laughed. "A lifetime of disapproval maybe." The moment those words fell from Ram's lips, he felt his heart squeeze and eyes start to sting at the same time. He froze, paralyzed with a fear that he might cry tears in front of his father. He began to silently beg his body not to betray him.

Ethelred watched his son closely for a time. "Disapproval of thin's you did is no' the same thin' as disapproval of you."

"Feels the same, sounds the same, looks the

same."

He sighed deeply. "Aye. Maybe so. I admit it bothers me to know you've spent your life believin' I do no' care for you." He got up, stirred the fire, and offered Ram a whiskey, which he accepted. "Rammel, let me ask you this. Have you no' noticed how much you are like your mother?"

Ram cocked his head. "You mean that my looks favor her? Aye. 'Tis inescapable."

"No. No' just looks. That you *are* alike. You and your mum, to some extent your sister, too. Tepring is everythin' I'm no'. Colorful. Excitin'. So alive you can almost see currents of electricity sparkin' off her. She's the very essence of what it means to be alive."

Ethelred had an expression on his face that could almost be called dreamy describing the queen. Ram had never heard his father talk about feelings before. He knew his parents were devoted to each other. He hadn't been entirely sure they were in love, not until that moment.

"I think she's the most marvelous creature to e'er walk on earth. Now tell me, how could I think so highly of her and, findin' you much the same, no' like you, Rammel?"

Ram couldn't have been more shocked by that confession if his father had admitted to wanting a sex change operation. He rose quickly and went to look out the window because he felt a tear spilling out of his eye. He swore to himself that, if he made it out of that situation with his dignity intact, he would never tease Elora about her crying again. Not now that he knew how hard it could be to control those impulses.

When he had himself under control, he swiped at his surreptitiously and turned back to his father.

"Thank you for sayin' so, Da. 'Twas very good to hear. Still, you and I both know I'm no' the right person for that job. 'Tis you. You were tryin' to do the noble thin', tryin' to see that your first son had his chance. 'Tis a shame that…" He decided that didn't need to be said. His father was already steeping in self-recrimination. "'Tis you, Da. No' me. Be king of elves. Make peace with the fae. Bless the union with Duff Torquil and brin' Song home."

Ethelred pressed his lips together. "That will no' work."

"Why no'?"

"Because I'm no' well." Ram opened his mouth to ask about it, but his father waved off the inquiry. "Oh. I will likely live long enough to erect a peace with the fae, but no' until Helm is king. Then we would be back where we are now. Aelsblood does no' have the character, Rammel. No' the character. And no' the honor to do the job as it needs doin'. Must be you."

"Just hold on. There are too many absurdities flyin' about the room. First off, Helm king? I'm pretty sure his mum and da do no' know a thin' about that and just as sure they would no' approve. Next, what's wrong with you, Da?"

Ethelred waved his hand. "Let's no' get sidetracked. We have much more important thin's to talk about."

"Mum knows?"

"'Aye. 'Tis part of the reason why she has a hanky permanently attached to the end of her arm."

"I ne'er knew you were in love with each other. No' in a romantic way."

"Oh, aye. Knowin' death is no' just an abstract concept makes you sentimental I suppose. I love your mum more than 'tis possible to say in words. 'Tis how you feel about your mate?"

"Aye. Maybe if Blood was mated, this whole thin' would have been different. Elora is the one who pointed out to me that Song and Duff feel that way about each other. She made me promise to do what I could to help them by sayin', 'What if it was us?'"

"When she made you promise to do what you could, do you think that included becomin' king of Ireland?"

Ram's heart dropped like it was made of lead. The one thing Elora had always insisted on was that she could never survive palace life again. It had been less than a year and a half since he'd promised her that she wouldn't have to, that she would never have to so much as set foot inside the palace if she didn't want to. How could he have imagined in a thousand years that the Fates might contrive a way to make him be forsworn? Honor indeed.

"No. It definitely did no'. But she loves Song," he said absently. He turned toward Ethelred. "I might like to ask Mr. Kilter a couple of questions if you think he would be so kind as to make the trip back over."

"I believe he could be persuaded." Ethelred rose to make the call.

"While you're doin' that, I'm goin' to step out and say good mornin' to my wife."

Elora was still in her tank top and pajama bottoms, telling Helm stories while feeding him baby oatmeal, when the phone rang.

"It's your dad, kiddo." Helm didn't look interested in anything except what the spoon was doing next. "Hey. What's the word?"

"Hey, yourself. Word is I miss you. Do no' like sleepin' alone."

"Same here."

"What are you doin'?"

"Feeding oatmeal to your son. Telling him stories now before he's old enough to call them stupid."

"Ah. So you're sittin' down then."

"I'm guessing that's a prelude to bad news."

"Well, aye."

"Has something happened to Song?"

"I'm guessin' you have no' seen the comment Blood made to the press on his way from leavin' the meetin' with Torquil? The one where he basically said our sister is on her own and no' really welcome back and he has no interest in peace with fae?'

Elora was stunned speechless. Almost. "That's just impossible, isn't it? I mean he's no fun, but I didn't take him for a bad person. Not like this."

"No' like this. No one expects the person holdin' the knife to be her own brother."

"I don't know what to say. How are your parents taking this?"

"Em, that's why I'm calling."

Ram explained all that had transpired in as

much detail as he could recall then he paused. When she said nothing, he lowered his voice. "Elora, I would no' put you in the position of havin' to decide if there was a choice, but I made you a promise and will no' break it. No' e'en for my sister. I can no' find a painless solution here, but I have thought of somethin' that might be a compromise.

"Would you want to hear it?"

"Yes."

"Da has no' told me what is ailin' him. He says only that he believes he will live long enough to see a transition to peace, but no' long enough to see Helm king."

"Helm? King? Rammel!"

"I know. I know. But this is what I'm thinkin'."

Ram was walking outside on a terrace when he saw Mr. Kilter arrive. He said goodbye to Elora and hurried back.

"Mr. Kilter, sorry to trouble you to return so soon."

"No' at all, my lord. Happy to do it."

"I believe my son, Rammel, has another question or two. Same terms as before. Do you agree?"

"Certainly, sir."

Kilter turned to Ram with the eagerness of a hobby puzzler receiving a new monthly in the mail.

"Mr. Kilter, my question concerns the possible succession of my son, who is on the cusp of emergin' from infancy. Hypothetically speakin', would it no' be possible for my father to name his grandson king, but appoint a regent to ask in his place until he's twenty-five?"

"Aye."

"Would it be possible to appoint himself as that regent with a contingency that I would be next in line to act as regent in the event of his death or incapacitation?"

"Aye."

"Thank you. And, last, would it be possible for my son to decline, to name someone else ruler on the occasion of his twenty-fifth birthday?"

Kilter looked at Ethelred then back at Ram. "Aye."

"What steps would need to be taken to legally dethrone my brother?"

"Legally? Why nothin' more than a public announcement by your father," he looked at Ethelred, "the king."

Ram smiled. "Aye, Mr. Kilter, I can appreciate your sentiment. There are many of us who see my father's face when we think 'king'. So the new arrangement would be effective at the time of a public announcement?"

"Aye, sir."

"Thank you." Ram looked at his father. "That's all I have for him at present."

Ethelred thanked Kilter again for returning and showed him to the door.

"Would those terms be agreeable to you, Da?"

"I'm thinkin' you're sellin' yourself short, lad. You'd make a fine king."

Ram grinned. "Hearin' that is worth more to

me than I can say, but bein' an improvement o'er Blood does no' make someone a fine king."

Ethelred made the announcement to a television news crew on the palace lawn with Ram standing behind him and quickly made arrangements to resume peace talks the following day.

When Aelsblood's jet landed, he was surprised to see so many representatives of the press crowding around the gates of the hangar. While still on the plane, his people were fielding calls asking how he felt about being removed from office.

Tepring came downstairs with a smile and without a handkerchief. She walked straight to Ethelred and put her arms around him. For a long time they hugged, gently swaying like they were slow dancing. Ram wondered how he could have missed the affection between them, realizing it must have always been there to be seen.

The three of them were in Ethelred's study talking about the future.

"Why the provision that Helm can appoint someone in his place?"

"Because," Ram began, "first and most obvious, he may no' want it. Second, if all goes well over the next twenty-five years, elves and fae may be ready to form a commonwealth. And who could better serve to reunite us than a grandchild of yours and the Scotia crown?"

Ethelred and Tepring were each thinking about the privilege of being part of such a sweeping change that would stand for the good of future generations. The moment came and went quickly when Aelsblood entered. He closed the door and leaned back against it looking first at Rammel, then at their mother, and finally at Ethelred.

"A public announcement, Da? You might have at least told me in private and saved me the humiliation."

"Was that no' a public announcement you made a few hours ago in which you called your sister a traitor and said she was no' motivation enough to cause you to talk to the Scotia king about a peace between us? I thought 'tis how we do thin's under your regime, Aelsblood. If you'll excuse us, we were just goin' to dinner. As a family."

He stepped away from the door and let them pass by. Ram didn't bother to try and hide his contempt.

CHAPTER 14

Ritavish Torquil and Ethelred Mag Lehane Hawking stood together in amiable agreement as they waited to sign the document in front of them. One of the things that Ms. Logature had done for them that was most helpful was to suggest they hire Idelman and Company, a New York public relations firm, to help them sell the new age to their own people.

Idelman and Co. proved to be worth every penny. Within twenty-four hours they had spun the event as the greatest love story the world had ever seen, the love that overcame a two-thousand-year-old conflict. Overnight, an industry of products, tours, and clubs featuring Song and Duff sprang into being including some scams promising tickets to the wedding. Idelman and Co. made sure the news media in Scotia and Ireland carried positive stories about how the fortunate mating was benefitting the GNP of both countries and how the celebrity of the couple had brought them under the global spotlight.

Between the documentary outlining the true history of the race and a powerful global wave of affection for the young couple, most fae and elves began to state publicly that they'd had private misgivings about the prejudice. "I'd been questionin' the sense of the thin' for a long while," was a commonly voiced sentiment when elves and fae were stopped on the street and asked how they felt about the end of hostilities.

Etana, in her guise as Arles Logature, approached the Eskildsens, owners of a guest house in the Faroes that had enjoyed the privilege of hosting the famous couple. She explained that the pair had actually been in their guest cottage the entire time and offered to pay the bill at three times the going rate. She also mentioned that the guest house could expect a deluge of reservations requests for having housed the royal celebrities and that they would have all the business they could manage for whatever price they'd like to charge for a while.

Mr. Eskildsen responded that, at his age, he got dates confused sometimes. If the young couple said they'd been guests, then who was he to argue? He created an invoice and thanked Ms. Logature for settling the bill.

"What would you do for me?"

For the sake of diversion Song and Duff had been to the village a couple of times and met interesting people with stories to match, but mostly they had spent their "honeymoon" reveling in the exhilarating pleasure of simply being together. After the first couple of days of solitude, they had fallen into the habit of doing without clothes. They found that perpetual access to each other's bodies only added to the euphoria of their reclusive love nest. It had been a time of companionable joy and seductive amusement, a euphoric bliss that was as intoxicating as any drug.

Their awareness of the illusory quality of their days and the likely transience of the experience only heightened their determination to suck every morsel of delight from every moment.

Duff looked up at Aelsong who was straddling him. He was lying on the little grass knoll that sloped down to the stream that ran beside the house. The air was heavy with the scent of blooming flowers and the grass felt cool and soft against his skin.

He raised an eyebrow and grinned as he trailed his fingertips slowly down between her bare breasts. "Are you hidin' a dragon for me to slay?"

"Oh, no. The dragons are all gone away. Except for my brother."

"Your brother, the king, or your brother, the hero?"

She laughed. "Aelsblood. I tried to kill him myself."

"When?"

"After they brought me home and he said I was goin' to be locked away."

"What did you do?"

"I picked up one of those old-fashioned iron pokers, the heavy kind, and swung it at his head."

Duff stared at her for a couple of beats and then started laughing. "I would have loved to have seen that. What did he do?"

"Well, first, he said, 'Ouch'."

Duff laughed so hard at that he had to sit up. He put his arms around her waist and adjusted her position while she put her arms around his neck.

Face to face, he said, "And then what?"

"Then he called the guards to drag me away. I

told him he'd better no' ever let me out or I'd kill him for sure the next time."

"I will take this as a cautionary tale, love. I'm renewin' my pledge to remain true to your good graces. I'm also makin' a new pledge to keep the pokers locked away when we are established in our own home."

Song's smile died away at that. "Our own home? 'Tis hard to guess where we may end."

"I do no' care so long as you're with me and no' tryin' to kill me."

The giggle that bubbled up was smothered by a kiss so lovely that she was happy to give up the laughter in sacrifice. There was growing evidence between her legs that Duff was taking the conversation in a new direction. As his kisses trailed down her neck he moved his hands to the sides of her breasts and lifted her at the same time. In a dance of mutual understanding as old as time, she reached between them to perfectly position his cock at her entrance and then sank slowly down. As she lowered herself, she pulled air in a gasp, let her head drop back, and finally brought her gaze back to watch his face as she whispered his name, "Duffy."

In the throes of the most powerful intimacy possible, his concentration on her reactions was so intense that it was a rapture almost painful. Song moved slowly, deliberately, erotically to heighten the sensations. Just as slowly, Duff's hands moved lightly over her body, his fingers greedy for the next touch before the last was complete. When Song began to move faster, increasing the friction, Duff's arousal kept pace.

He came up to his knees while holding her in place so that he could get more leverage. Holding her in a tight embrace, with arms wrapped around her, he pulled almost all the way out and plunged into her with a thrust so purposeful it could only be called ravishment. Hearing her responding cry spurred him on to pumping in a merciless triumph of claiming. He adjusted her position once more so that her most sensitive nerve endings would be brushed by the piston motion between them. Within a few seconds, he felt her squeezing him and let go in a seizure of ecstasy that can only be known by species that mate.

They stayed in that position, panting. He held her close with one arm while he reached up and used the other hand to brush the damp hair back from her face. Keeping his hand against her cheek, he angled her head back a little so that she was looking at him. "I love you, Song."

She swallowed and felt her heart clinch in her chest. Her beautiful kiss-swollen lips parted so that she could say it back, but her throat closed and she felt a tear run down her face instead.

"Here now. What's this?" He wiped one wet trail away with his thumb.

She nodded, then shook her head, and then flapped her hands until she could find her voice. "Is this what matin' does? I'm goin' to be as bad as Elora with the silly weepin'."

"She has a reputation for tears, does she?"

"Aye," Song laughed. "She does. But that was no' what I intended to be sayin'. What I meant to be sayin' is, I love you, too, Duffy. We're goin' to be okay, whate'er 'tis that comes next."

"O'course. I proclaim it. Also, as to what I would do for you. I will murder your brother if you wish it, but 'twould surely mean war, *actual* war, between your people and mine."

She seemed to contemplate that. "You're goin' to have to retrain yourself to stop thinkin' in terms of your people and mine. 'Tis our people now. And, no, love. I release you from the charge. If he needs killin' badly enough, I'll do it myself," she smiled just as the doorbell rang.

"Did you hear a doorbell?"

"Aye. I think 'twas the tune of 'Comin' Through the Rye'."

They got up and walked to the cottage, looked around the front door, but there was no sign of a doorbell.

"Maybe 'tis the angel tryin' to be polite and give us a chance to make ourselves presentable before he appears."

"Let's go with that," said Song.

They pulled on clothes and sat down to wait for a visitor with fruity beverages.

A few minutes later Kellareal arrived to explain all that had happened. They looked at each other and each knew what the other was thinking – that there was a sadness in giving up the paradise they had enjoyed, wherever it was. Whatever it was.

Duff reached for Song's hand. "So we're the greatest love story e'er told."

"Already knew that."

Duff smiled at her like she was made for him,

which, of course, she was. "Life goes on, I suppose."

"So they say."

Kellareal went on with the briefing. "The plan is to deposit you in the little cottage on the Faroes. We have also arranged to have your plane, with all your things in it, returned to the air field there. You will fly back to Edinburgh and be greeted by the subjects who are eager to give you an enthusiastic welcome."

"When?"

"How long do you need to get ready?"

"'Tis no' that 'twould take long. 'Tis that we do no' want to leave. Could we have one more night?"

Kellareal's features seem to soften a little. "Tomorrow morning then. Early."

Song nodded. Duff sighed, picked up the hand he was holding and kissed the back of it.

They took off from the airstrip on the Faroe Islands, but instead of returning to Aberdeen, they flew directly to Edinburgh. Just as the angel had predicted, an enormous crowd was gathered outside the gates to the private hangars where small aircraft were housed.

There was a sizable security guard and motorcade as well as a small roped off area for TV crew and news people. When Duff switched the engine off and turned to look at Song, he thought he saw a hint of panic behind her eyes. The echo of their experience in Quebec brought a mutual fear of being separated bubbling to the surface. He couldn't blame her for the suspicion and hesitation, especially not when his own feelings mirrored hers. He gave her hand a squeeze and she responded with a smile that was brave, if not genuine. It was a marvel to him that he already knew her that well after so short a time.

"Stay where you are, love. I'll circle 'round and help you out so that you can make a proper entrance."

She nodded. "Just a second."

He saw that she reached under her skirt, seemingly to make an adjustment to some article of clothing in the area of her crotch.

Duff waved at the cheering crowd on his way around to the other side of the plane. Aelsong gave him her left hand to help her out of the plane and touched his lips with a light kiss saying, "Looks like a warm enough welcome."

She reached up with her right hand, presumably to wipe lipstick from his mouth, but what she did instead was to touch the indentation above his upper lip with mating scent. His nostrils flared, his eyes widened and his entire frame tensed.

They were ushered past the hand-selected members of the press on the way to the waiting cars. Security allowed them to stop in front of the reporters.

"Your Highness, how does it feel to be comin' home with an elf bride?"

Song looked at Duff, who seemed to have experienced a brain freeze. She could tell by the expression on his face that he was far from fully present in the moment. Fortunately, she had spent a fair amount of time in the public eye and was comfortable with attention. "There's a wee frog in his throat this mornin', so he can no' say and I would no' want to presume to answer for him. But I can say that I'm so happy to be in this beautiful city with the man I love."

"Princess Hawking, what do you think about your nephew bein' named king of Ireland?"

She smiled. "Well, I can assure you there has ne'er been an Irish king who was cuter or chubbier." Everyone laughed. "And I can no' tell you how delighted I am to have my da actin' in the capacity of head of state." She looked over at Duff. "When I saw our two fathers on the tele together, I thought they looked so handsome, like a symbol of our peoples reunitin', which is as it should be. We're the same."

"What are your plans?"

"We're open. What are yours?"

There was more laughter. The news people clearly loved her and had more questions ready, but the king's staff pressed them on toward the cars.

As their vehicle pulled past the people lining the exit route, they saw hundreds of handmade signs with encouraging phrases like, "Welcome Home, Princess", and roses were being thrown at the limousine.

By the time they'd left the crowd behind, Duff had recovered his senses. He leaned into Song. "That was mean."

She put her lips close to his ear so only he would hear. "In my defense, I thought it would help you get through the nonsense. I honestly did no' know that it would paralyze your tongue."

He pulled back to look at her as if to judge her

truthfulness. "They adored you. Ate it up. So perhaps 'twas all for the best." She nodded. He smiled. "Still, I will be gettin' you back."

Her answering smile was the first time he had ever experienced the full frontal fireworks force of Hawking sparkle at close range. "You can try."

Ram came through the apartment door looking flushed with the excitement of being reunited with his little family. Elora had Helm in the highchair and was feeding him smashed peas.

"Is that the child who would be king?"

Helm waved his arms and kicked his feet while Elora stood and turned to greet her mate. "No. That's just a spoiled baby with peas on his face."

Ram pulled her tight into the sort of welcome home kiss that let her know he wasn't joking about being glad to be back. When they drew apart, he kept his forehead against hers and talked in the tone he normally reserved for bed.

"Missed you."

"How much?"

Helm had been as patient as he could with his parents' intermission. He didn't cry or whine. He didn't scream. He yelled a demand for more food at the top of his lungs and there was no mistaking his meaning. He even turned red in the face to punctuate the gravity of the situation. Ram and Elora both stared at him.

"Wow. It didn't take long for that to go to his

head. Just *one* mention of being king," she said. "Exactly what I told you."

"Oh," Ram laughed, "'cause neither one of us has e'er been the least insistent about gettin' what we want when we want it. Stop lookin' for trouble, Mum." Ram went to the refrigerator, withdrew a jar of baby meat sticks, and put three on his son's tray. "Put a meat stick in it and let your da have his way with her for a minute, will ye?" He turned back to Elora, smiling. "Did I mention there's no place like home?"

For more on Victoria's books visit my website, **www.VictoriaDanann.com** or my blog at **http://victoriadanann.me.**

To all of you who have helped make this serial saga a success, I am so humbled and so grateful to be able to spend my days spinning tales.

The Witch in the Woods,
Victoria Danann

You're always welcome to write.
vdanann@gmail.com